STUDENT BODY

Bev Bachmann

◆ FriesenPress

Suite 300 - 990 Fort St
Victoria, BC, V8V 3K2
Canada

www.friesenpress.com

Copyright © 2017 by Bev Bachmann
First Edition — 2017

All rights reserved.

No part of this publication may be reproduced in any form, or by any means, electronic or mechanical, including photocopying, recording, or any information browsing, storage, or retrieval system, without permission in writing from FriesenPress.

ISBN
978-1-5255-0587-4 (Hardcover)
978-1-5255-0588-1 (Paperback)
978-1-5255-0589-8 (eBook)

1. FICTION, MYSTERY & DETECTIVE

Distributed to the trade by The Ingram Book Company

To Sharon (and Frank)
I hope you enjoy this one!

Bev Bachmann

Table of Contents

1	"A big test?"	1
2	Hapless Characters	11
3	The Distraction	14
4	Coffee Break	19
5	Buzz and Fuzz	26
6	A Case of Murder	36
7	The Staff Meeting	43
8	Salad and Sorrow	47
9	Perogies and Pain	52
10	Tourtiere and Temptation	59
11	Ravioli and Regrets	64
12	Pizza and Promises	73
13	Scallops and Scandal	78
14	"Typical teenage stuff."	84
15	Power Trippers	91
16	The Wayward Coaster	95
17	Magda	102
18	"A force of nature"	111
19	At Police Headquarters	116
20	Fiats and Ferraris	124

21	Tools of the Trade	131
22	Mary D'Agosta	139
23	"The LED doesn't lie"	145
24	Shop Talk, Part 1	148
25	Julie Gauvin	155
26	Checkmate	163
27	Shop Talk, Part II	165
28	Setting the Stage	170
29	Dragon Lady	176
30	Smoke and Mirrors	180
31	"They should have been there."	189
32	The Long Night	197
33	The Trap	200
34	Hour of Reckoning, Part I	203
35	Girl Talk	211
36	Hour of Reckoning, Part II	216
37	"Arrest the bastard!"	223
38	The Competition	229
39	Collateral Damage	236
40	"A beaker full of acid"	245
EPILOGUE		251
Two Weeks Later		251

MONDAY

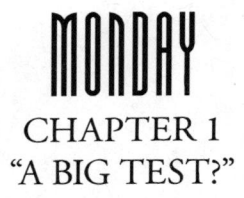

CHAPTER 1
"A BIG TEST?"

6:17 a.m.

Christmas break was over and staff at Fairmont High were returning to school after a two-week vacation. The air was bitterly cold, even for January, and the storm that had been threatening to arrive for days was rapidly approaching.

First year teacher Julie Gauvin pulled her small silver Toyota into the parking lot adjacent to a large empty field owned by the board of education. As she trudged through the blinding snowfall, a fierce wind was whipping at her back, but that didn't matter to Julie. At long last she was in a job she loved and no amount of miserable weather was going to dampen her enthusiasm. Even before she had left for school that morning, she had already decided – today was going to be a good day.

It was still dark when the young teacher reached the safety of her portable and stepped inside. Shoving the door closed against an onslaught of flying snow, she walked briskly to the front and, without taking off her coat, sat on the edge of her desk to get an overview of her classroom. It was not a pretty sight.

Normally the caretaking staff left before night school classes began, leaving her with a mess to clean up the next morning. However, since the school was going to be empty for two weeks during the Christmas break, she had hoped they would have made an exception this time.

They hadn't.

Desktops were still sticky from drinks that had been spilled two weeks earlier, and a thick coating of chalk dust blanketed the blackboard. Adding to the chaos, desks had been shoved every which way by students making a mad dash to the door the minute night class was over.

Earlier in the previous September, Julie made an effort to remedy the situation by repeatedly leaving polite notes for the night school teacher, but to no avail. Finally she felt compelled to complain to the administration and was informed a messy room was not high on their list of priorities. In the end, she concluded that if she wanted something done, it was up to her to do it.

And that was how she ended up arriving at her portable at 6:30 each morning when, in fact, the school day officially began at 8:15.

Showing up for work that early actually turned out to have unexpected advantages. After cleaning up her room, Julie was left with plenty of time to mark papers, make lesson plans, or simply sit and settle her mind in preparation for the demands of the day ahead.

She understood that, unlike her, Fairmont students didn't have the same luxury of a warm comfortable place in which to wait until 8:15. Early arrivals had two options. They could hang around in the popular, but crowded, cafeteria or else they could look for a space to settle in the school's small, stuffy library.

So one morning early in the fall, she announced to all her classes that, although she would be arriving much sooner, she would allow them to camp out in her portable starting at 7:45 as long as they were quiet and respectful of each other's space—including hers. And for several months it had worked out well.

Until today.

But now it was time to roll up her sleeves and get to work. First, she fished a wet rag out of a plastic bag in her backpack and cleaned the blackboard with long horizontal strokes until it shone like new. Then she gave each of the desktops a swipe before lining them up into tidy symmetrical rows.

Her caretaking chores completed, she stepped back to survey her handiwork with the scrutiny of a general inspecting her troops. Julie couldn't help but smile. Everything was perfect.

Outside the snowstorm was picking up speed, and the portable walls began to shake as if seized by a giant hand. Startled, Julie looked towards the front door which held the room's only window. For an instant, she thought she saw a face peering back at her, but she couldn't be sure. It might have been real, but then again, through the thick curtain of falling snow, it might have been a mirage. She took a second look, and this time the vision was gone. Julie shrugged. Real or not, she still had work to do. Time was running out.

The last item on her agenda was to set out an array of color-coded folders along the outer edge of her desk. Her mind was on *Macbeth*, the play she was introducing that day, and the sound of the wind whirling around the portable walls made her think of the play's three witches flying around the world in an endless search for ways to stir up trouble.

In fact, the weather was in such sync with the mood of the play, Julie actually welcomed the storm's pounding away at her poorly built portable. She couldn't have asked for a more perfect day to begin a play about forces of evil wreaking havoc in the world of mortals.

Her preparations almost complete, Julie glanced at the clock and noted it was now 6:50. An uneasy feeling gripped her. She wasn't overly concerned, but it did make her wonder. She knew she was comfortable with public speaking. No, it wasn't speaking in front of a class that had her spooked. It was something else. Whatever it was, Julie would have to ignore it because in precisely 55 minutes students needing a place to study could start showing up, and that was a reality she couldn't ignore.

Student Body

An unexpected blast of Arctic air burst into the room and with it a tall Italian boy with thick black curls dusted with snowflakes which he shook onto the portable floor.

"Hey, teach! Mind if I come in?" he said, grinning roguishly. "I know I'm supposed to wait until 7:45, but I got a big test coming up, and I really need to study. Is that okay?"

Julie looked up from her desk with some annoyance. "A big test? On the first day back at school?!" Julie wasn't a suspicious person by nature, but this sounded a bit fishy to her. "Couldn't you have studied *during* the Christmas break? You had two weeks in which to prepare."

"Yeah, well," he shrugged. "You know how it is."

Julie sighed. She *did* know 'how it is' with teenagers—especially this one. "Okay, you can come in," she said somewhat reluctantly, "as long as you're quiet."

The boy hurried to a desk in the front row and threw off his jacket. "Thanks," he said, sitting down and opening a sizable textbook. "You're a life saver."

Julie wasn't pleased with this intrusion into her personal time, but it was about what she could expect from DiAngelo "Dino" D'Agosta, the student who was consistently late to her period five class—and not by accident.

Dino got a kick out of knowing all the girls were following him with their eyes as he casually sauntered to his seat. Julie often had to put her lesson on hold until he was finally settled at his desk before she could continue.

She might have called him out on it, but that would have given him more of the attention he wanted. So she ignored him. It was a quick and pointed way of communicating that she didn't take the boy all that seriously.

However, that was not the case for the teenage girls in her class, and to be fair, Julie couldn't really blame them. Dino was drop dead gorgeous. But brains? That was another story.

For months she had heard rumors that Dino got by on his looks alone and that it wasn't just the females in Fairmont's student body who fell under his spell. She wasn't sure if the rumors were true, and frankly, she didn't care. She was far too busy being a first-year teacher to be sidetracked by salacious gossip.

Julie forgot about the boy as she focused on her final housekeeping detail—replacing the tiny nubs of chalk with fresh finger length pieces. Now and then she felt eyes staring at her back as she progressed along the length of the blackboard tray, but each time she turned around, Dino's head was bent over his textbook as if absorbed in reading. She continued with her work. Time was getting away.

An unexpected clicking sound caught Julie's attention. She turned around to see Dino staring out the portable window with his hand poised on the door's lock. In a flash, he whirled around.

Julie watched in astonishment as the boy began advancing in her direction, his pace quickening with each step. And he wasn't stopping.

Student Body

She wasn't afraid, just surprised. Nothing like this had ever been covered in any of her courses at the Faculty of Education. However, she did remember a professor once commenting that whenever a teacher was confronted with a potential crisis, the safest thing to do was to act with authority. That was supposed to defuse the situation—hypothetically. Now that a boy with the body of a man was striding rapidly towards her, Julie decided it was a good time to test that theory.

"What are you doing?" she demanded sternly. "Get back to your seat!"

Dino grasped her firmly by the shoulders. "C'mon, teach," he sneered, "I've seen the looks you've been giving me in class. I know what those looks mean. No one likes a cocktease, Julie."

It was the mention of her given name that stunned her more than anything. It sent her mind reeling.

"We've got close to 45 minutes before anyone shows up," he said with a knowing wink. "Let's not waste time."

Julie couldn't believe what she was hearing. This kid had to be clear out of his mind! She tried to look around for some kind of weapon, but his body was blocking her line of sight. He was now so close she could smell the sickly sweet aroma of his aftershave.

"Get the hell out of here!" she ordered. "Before I call the cops."

"The cops?" Dino laughed. "Who'd believe you? The door is locked, and we're in here alone. Furthermore," he smirked, "it's your word against mine."

Her heart began to race. She needed to think, but there wasn't time. Dino's breath was fanning her face. He moistened his lips and began lowering his head until his mouth was practically on top of hers. Julie froze in horror.

At the last second, she turned her head sharply to the right as his kiss skimmed her cheek. Then, for one infinitesimal moment, he paused, and in that moment Julie cast a quick look around. And there, sitting on the corner of her desk, she caught sight of the snow globe, a treasured souvenir from a long-ago trip to Niagara Falls with her late mother.

Dino started hyperventilating. As he tightened his grasp of her shoulders, something hard was beginning to pulsate against her groin. *Now* she was scared. This wild eyed, sexually charged adolescent had one thing on his mind. Nothing she had learned at the faculty could help her now.

Julie was finding it hard to breathe, but unlike Dino, it wasn't from passion. She counted on the boy's arrogance to convince him otherwise.

"Dino," she said breathlessly, "a condom?"

"Why, Julie," he grinned. "what a practical girl you are." He loosened his grip for just a second to slip his hand into his pants pocket.

That was all the time she needed.

Student Body

Stretching her free arm towards the edge of her desk, she seized the snow globe and smashed it hard against the side of his head.

The boy stumbled backwards and latched onto a school desk to steady himself. Soon a tiny thread of red spread from his temple down to the cut of his jaw. For a moment he seemed stunned, but then he focused a look of loathing on the teacher standing behind her desk as if it offered a protective barrier. She was watching him closely.

"You bitch!" he snarled, touching the dampness at his temple. He held his bloodied hand up to his face. "You'll pay for this!"

His eyes bored into her, and for a brief moment, Julie wondered if he was going to come after her again. She held her breath and waited. But then he grabbed his jacket and started weaving his way towards the back of the room, crashing into desk after desk along the way. When he reached the door, he violently yanked it open before lurching outside where the shrieking wind welcomed him with a fearsome embrace.

And then he was gone.

—

Julie's mind was racing. What if Dino decided to return and finish what he started? She ran to the door, locked it, then returned to her desk and sat quietly to clear her head.

What she really needed to do was to go to the washroom in the main building where she could splash cold water on her face in an effort to regain her composure. After a few minutes, she looked out the door window and confirmed that other teachers were arriving. Glancing at the clock, she calculated that, if she hustled, she could make it to the washroom in the main building and be back in her portable roughly ten minutes before the first students were permitted to enter her portable. Hurriedly she pulled on her boots and grabbed her coat.

She was half way to the door when she remembered Dino's textbook was still sitting on his desk. Someone was bound to ask about it, and she wasn't in the mood for questions. The nasty business of the morning was something that she would deal with later when she had the luxury of time.

Reaching for Dino's book, she spotted the snow globe lying on its side. There was a fleck of something on the smooth convex surface. She didn't need to examine it. She knew what it was.

She wrapped a tissue around the glass ball and slipped it into the bottom drawer of her desk alongside Dino's trigonometry textbook.

Now there was no time to lose. Throwing her coat over her shoulders, she sprinted to the portable door and started running across the parking lot—the howling wind dogging her every step.

CHAPTER 2
HAPLESS CHARACTERS

8:15 a.m.

After a brief introduction to *Macbeth*, which Julie thought went well - all things considered -- she started the class on seat work. That hadn't been her original plan for the day, but she had to get people working quietly at their desks so the focus wouldn't be all on her. A teacher never knew when she was being surreptitiously studied, and Julie couldn't afford to have some sensitive soul picking up on tell-tale signs all was not right with her world.

She began by walking up and down rows, handing out assignment sheets.

"Answers will be put on the board first thing tomorrow," she announced breezily, "but if you apply yourselves, you can be finished before the end of the period, and then there won't be any homework."

Her voice was light, almost carefree. She wondered if she didn't deserve an Oscar for her performance.

Unaware of their teacher's inner turmoil, students began blithely opening their books. Julie couldn't help but smile as she watched them. After the rough encounter with Dino that morning, she'd had to call on all her teacher tricks to appear as natural as she had on any other day. And it worked!

You're a cool customer, Julie Gauvin, she thought, giving herself a mental pat on the back while strolling from desk to desk, stopping here and there to check on her students' progress.

The peaceful atmosphere in the room gave Julie some much needed relief from tension, but all too soon the calmness was shattered by the sound of sirens in the distance growing louder and louder until it seemed as if they might crash through the thin portable walls at any minute. All eyes turned nervously towards the door.

That was Julie's cue to get up and march confidently across the room. She opened the door slightly and took a quick look around but didn't see anything unusual through the falling snow which had started to ease off.

"Everything's okay," she said as she pulled the door closed behind her. "Continue with your work."

Gradually students returned to their assignments.

With her class working quietly, Julie could now allow herself to think about her next move. She had basically three options. She could wait until her spare to go to the office and report what had happened; she could excuse herself now and do it immediately; or she could wait until later in the day when she had time to think rationally before making a decision. She decided on the last option.

Having settled on a course of action, Julie suddenly found her imagination going into overdrive.

What if Dino had been out there stumbling around in the parking lot when one of the other teachers had arrived and offered to take the boy to the office? And when Dino told his story, what would he say? She was the teacher – the adult in the situation. Wouldn't she bear most of the responsibility for a seemingly serious conflict with a student?

Julie shivered. It struck her that any scenario provided by the boy would probably cast her in a bad light, and there wasn't much she could do about it. She might even lose her job. Ironically, she thought, she was now in a similar situation to any one of the hapless characters in the play she was about to introduce.

The blood-soaked *Macbeth*.

CHAPTER 3
THE DISTRACTION

9:15 a.m.

"Mid-terms will be coming up soon, so let's see how much you remember from before the Christmas Break," Elaine Richardson announced as students started filing into her classroom. "All right now. Books closed, desks cleared."

After a bit of shuffling, students found their seats and sat down quickly. Some were a little apprehensive, but most were fairly confident. They had learned to trust their math teacher, even if she was from a completely different generation.

At 62, Elaine was the oldest teacher on staff. During the previous five years, she had thought often about retiring, but she was torn. Elaine loved math the way Beethoven must have loved music or Hemingway, writing, and it was a lot to give up. Not only that, but this year she had some particularly bright students in her trigonometry class—young people who were bound to end up at the top of their chosen professions. Such students were a joy to teach.

On the other hand, she was getting low on physical energy, and standing on her feet all day was starting to wear her down. If she were to retire, she would be absolved of all responsibilities, even the ones at home since her last child had married and moved out of the house five years ago. After that, she and her husband had had the kind of privacy that allowed them to rekindle their romance, and rekindle it they did—in every room of the house.

Then fate in the form of a fatal stroke robbed her of the love of her life, and she was at a loss as to what to do with herself. So she kept on doing the thing she knew best, teaching. Besides a discomfiting sense of loneliness was starting to seep into her life. At least at school she had the companionship of her colleagues. She wasn't ready to give that up yet.

"Does this count?" A voice from somewhere in the back of the room caught her attention.

Kids these days were so mark conscious, she thought, shaking her head sadly. Nobody seemed interested anymore in learning for its own sake.

"Everything *counts*," she said crisply. Actually, she intended the quiz to act as a means of a review, but they didn't need to know that.

"Calculators are permitted, so go ahead and get them out," she said while strolling up and down the rows, placing a test paper face down on each desk. She reminded them not to turn their tests over until everyone had received a copy. Then she returned to the front of the room and turned to face them. "All right," she said brightly, "you may begin."

She parked herself on top of her desk and settled in. From her elevated position, she could view her entire class. That way it was easy to take attendance by scanning the room for empty seats. Only one person was missing.

Now that she had taken attendance, and her students were busily writing the 'test,' she could relax for a few minutes. With some classes, that simply wasn't possible. But with this group she could appear to be watching them, when, in fact, her mind was preoccupied with a myriad other thoughts. And the thought foremost on her mind today was of the boy who wasn't in his seat.

DiAngelo D'Agosta

—

When did he first appear in her life? Was it five or *six* weeks ago? She did remember that it was the first day of term two. He'd been standing in the doorway at the back of the room watching her for a full minute before taking a tentative step inside and choosing a seat as far away from the front as possible.

Elaine did not recognize him as he had never appeared in any of her previous classes—so she had no idea what to expect. However, one thing was immediately apparent. The boy was strikingly handsome with thick black curls and

Student Body

alluring brown eyes that often appeared to be studying her. That didn't particularly strike Elaine as unusual. She figured that, like a lot of students, he found the subject intimidating, and he was simply acting out of a sense of insecurity.

Dino's first marked assignment made clear that he lacked the most basic mathematic fundamentals. Elaine wondered how he had gotten into her advanced class in the first place. She knew that kids were often pushed through the system by ambitious administrators or misguided guidance counselors who wanted their school to look good. The end result was that a teacher could sometimes find herself stuck with students woefully unprepared to be taking her course. Typically, these students dropped out after the first test. Certainly the second test was make or break time. The results of his first test sent Dino to Elaine for after-school help.

It wasn't unusual for her to tutor kids, but this boy stood out as particularly keen. He was observant, respectful, and committed. By the end of the first week, Elaine found herself becoming fond of the Italian boy with the killer smile and the mischievous gleam in his eye. Of course, staying late at school meant she would have to face rush hour traffic, but that wasn't much of a sacrifice. With no one waiting for her at home, what was the point of hurrying to get there?

The boy's progress was steady but slow, and Elaine could see that he was motivated enough, but not very academically inclined. However, he had a knack for reading people, often with astonishing accuracy, and it didn't take him long to discover that his tutor was a woman with a big hole in her life. She was a mother with no children and a wife with no husband.

He couldn't have asked for a more perfect set-up.

—

"Mrs. Richardson?" A small voice from somewhere in the room pulled her back into the present.

"Yes?"

"What do we do when we're finished?"

"Get ready to go over the answers while I read the questions out loud, of course," she said authoritatively, as if she had been paying attention all along.

Actually Elaine was shocked by her own behavior. Losing track of what was going on, particularly during any kind of test, was unprofessional. Her only excuse—if she could call it that—was that she had been distracted by a missing boy who had been taking up way too much space in her head.

It wouldn't happen again.

CHAPTER 4
COFFEE BREAK

10:15 a.m.

It was her "on call", or spare period, and Magdalena Malinsky chose to spend it in the small staffroom rather than in the much larger one the teachers used mostly for socializing.

"On call" periods were assigned to every member of the staff as insurance against a teacher having to suddenly leave school for an emergency. However, this rarely happened, so most of the teachers considered their "on call" a free period. Since no teacher was absent on the first day back at school, Magda, who was head of the science department, knew she was in the clear. And that was good because the woman desperately needed some time to herself.

Her knees were aching and swollen due to the brutal weather, and she was tired. Achingly—deep in the bone—tired. She had hardly slept the night before, and now all she could think about was coffee -- good, strong, piping hot coffee.

She stood at the kitchenette's counter and poured herself a cup from the glass carafe that had been simmering all morning. The inky black liquid had almost completely evaporated, but there was just enough left for one more cup.

Magda dumped several packets of sugar and some weird looking white powder into the oily mix. She watched as it bubbled into tiny dough-like balls that started bouncing up and down as soon as the artificial creamer hit the scalding surface. It was rather grotesque, in a fascinating sort of way. Magda didn't care. Disgusting or not, it was coffee.

When Magda was a student at the University of Toronto, she had relied on a steady supply of caffeine in order to stay up all night. She had planned to enter medical school after getting her undergrad degree, and sleep deprivation was part of the price she was willing to pay to get there. Unfortunately, there were other challenges to consider.

The biggest one was Magda's sense of duty to her parents who had immigrated from the old country when Magda was twelve and then spent years struggling to survive in their adopted homeland.

Finally, after much hard work, the couple was able to purchase a small semi-detached in Parkdale and still finance their only child's university education. Unfortunately, these heavy expenses depleted most of their savings, and as Magda was about to graduate from U of T, her parents were considering taking out a second mortgage on their house.

She couldn't let that happen. So instead of proceeding with her original plans, she entered the Faculty of Education where she was able to earn a teacher's degree in a fraction of the time it would have taken her to qualify as a doctor.

When it came time to look for a job, Magda's excellent academic record meant she had her pick of schools. She chose Fairmont for no other reason than it was located within walking distance of her home in Parkdale. A bonus was the proliferation of European delicatessens she would pass along the way.

On the whole, Magda didn't regret her decision, but it hadn't been easy for her to forgo her dream of becoming a doctor. However, family came first, and her aging parents needed her. To further assist them, she continued to live at home and pay rent at the going rate for the city of Toronto.

The arrangement wasn't altogether a sacrifice. Magda really did love her parents and didn't mind living with them, but at the age of 44, this wasn't where she had seen her life going. There had been a time when she had dreams of having a home and a family of her own. Unfortunately, that never happened.

Her parents, who had always hoped for grandchildren, tried to do what they could by introducing her to available bachelors at their local church, but to no avail. She was big boned and plain looking, and no matter how she tried, she just couldn't seem to lose weight. She liked to blame a steady diet of her mother's special cottage cheese and potato perogies—not to mention huge helpings of blini heaped with homemade jam. But it had been a losing battle, and in time she came to accept that she was destined to be a heavyset girl with thick thighs and padded hips. Nature had designed her that way. Why fight it?

Perhaps if she had possessed a pretty face, men might have overlooked her other detractions, but that wasn't the case. Her skin tone was sallow, and she eschewed the use of cosmetics. It was a matter of pride. Magda felt that her intelligence should be enough for any man. In the Ukraine, the home of her ancestors, a woman with brains was highly prized. But this was Canada where beauty was considered capital. So she did what children of immigrants had been doing for decades. She made adjustments.

"Don't tell me you're *drinking* that awful stuff!"

Elaine Richardson had slipped unnoticed into the workroom, surprising Magda who was stirring her coffee in an abstract fashion.

"Have some of my green tea," Elaine suggested. "It's a lot better for you than that stuff."

Magda shook her head. She knew the older teacher meant well, but Magda didn't need another mother.

"Thanks all the same," she smiled wanly, "but this is my poison of preference."

She cradled her cup of coffee in her two hands and carried it carefully across the room to the worn-out tweed sofa where she sat down and closed her eyes—a gesture she hoped would hint that she wasn't in the mood to chat.

"To each her own," Elaine said cheerily.

She plugged the kettle in and pulled a canister down from one of the top shelves. It was an easy reach for the tall, thin teacher with neatly coiffed white hair and long slender fingers. She dropped her teabag into a clean cup and covered it with boiling water.

"Have you seen Gunther this morning? He usually drops by around eleven."

Magda moaned. So, there was to be no escape from small talk. "I don't know," she said. "Maybe he's outside having a smoke."

Elaine grabbed hold of the kettle and poured boiling water into her cup. Suddenly she turned to face the door. "Did you hear that?"

"Did I hear what?"

"It sounded like footsteps running down the hall. I think I'll take a look," she said, setting her cup of tea down on the counter and softly opening the door.

"Good idea," Magda said, leaning back against the sofa cushions and taking advantage of a few moments of quiet while Elaine was out of the room.

Soon the math teacher returned, flushed with excitement.

"I spoke to one of the secretaries, and she said there's a rumor someone found a body in that empty field beside the teacher parking lot." She stopped to catch her breath.

Magda frowned. "A *body*? Are you sure that's what she said?"

"Of course, I'm sure," Elaine said, a bit hurt at not being taken at her word.

Magda was silent. She needed a few minutes to process this information—if, indeed, it were true.

Elaine also had been thinking. Finally she came up with what she thought was a credible explanation.

"Maybe the body belongs to one of those homeless people in the neighborhood. He could have stumbled onto the school grounds during the night and then froze to death in the field," she speculated. "What do you think, Magda?"

"What do I think?" she repeated, setting her cup down on the coffee table. "I think we need to know more facts before we can draw any conclusions." She paused for a moment. "Anyway, I'm sure we'll find out more when Velma comes in."

"Well, she's the boss now, isn't she?" Elaine muttered under her breath.

"Did you say something?"

"Not really." Elaine looked away.

Magda raised a quizzical eyebrow but didn't pursue it.

Elaine suddenly had a troubling thought. "Magda, if it is a body, you don't think the person was *killed*, do you?"

"Well, the school is located in a dangerous neighborhood. It's entirely possible."

"I know that, but why would anyone want to attack someone on school grounds *and* in the middle of a blizzard? It just doesn't make any sense."

"That sort of thing never does," Magda replied.

"Killed?" Elaine repeated, her eyes widening. She was quiet for a moment as both women lapsed into silence.

"Magda?"

"Yes."

"You don't really believe that, do you?"

Magda lifted her coffee cup to her lips. "I don't know," she said, a whisper of worry in her voice. "I just have this feeling that what we're dealing with here is murder."

CHAPTER 5
BUZZ AND FUZZ

11:15 a.m.

It was now officially the lunch period, and Magda and Elaine decided to forgo the chaos of the school's cafeteria and remain in the small staff room.

A few minutes later, Julie came in and proceeded to the nearest chair and collapsed into it.

Both Magda and Elaine noticed but said nothing. Something heavy was obviously weighing the girl down, and the two older teachers decided to give her some space.

Just then, the door burst open, and Armand Saint-Yves, a small, wiry man with a grey pencil point goatee, stormed in and stood at the counter with his hands on his hips, glaring at the empty coffee pot as if it had personally offended him.

"Does anyone know where we keep the damn bags of coffee?" he demanded, opening and closing cupboard doors with a loud bang.

Student Body

"Try above the fridge," suggested Elaine.

"Yes, and stop making so much racket," Magda chimed in. "This is supposed to be the quiet staff room."

"Sorry, your highness," he said. "Far be it for me to disturb your rest."

Magda ignored him, but Elaine smiled softly as if she were indulging a petulant child. "Hard to get back in the groove after two weeks off, is it?"

In spite of his mercurial moods, or perhaps even because of them, she was rather fond of the flamboyant French teacher. He was fun and could be counted on to add a bit of colour to the day.

Armand began savagely tearing at an unopened bag of Folger's and filling the carafe with water from the sink. "How many more weeks until March Break?" he grumbled.

Julie stirred at the sound of water running. "You're making a fresh pot?" She managed a feeble smile. "I sure could use a cup?"

"Well, what else matters?" he said testily.

Magda had had enough. "Listen, Armand, no one is particularly happy about coming back to school, so let's at least try to be civil and not make this day any worse."

He stared at the cupboard door as if turning the matter over in his mind. "Listen, Julie," he said, turning to face her,

"I'm sorry I snapped. I'm just annoyed at having to be here. That's all."

Actually, Armand, whose real name was Arnold Schultz before he had it legally changed thirty years ago, was not altogether annoyed. He realized he was the focus of their attention, and few things in life gave him more pleasure. At one point during his university days, Armand had considered a career on the stage, but show business was a risky venture, so he opted for the field of education instead. It turned out to be a good move.

As a teacher, Armand had the security of a sizeable salary as well as some substantial benefits, such as free eyeglasses, coverage for physiotherapy, and all the dental work he wanted. Those things mattered, of course, but the real attraction for Armand was the fact that for five hours a day, five days a week, he had a captive audience. True, he was never going to see his name up in lights on Broadway, but a person has to be practical. There were enough uncertainties in life as it was.

"Anyway," Armand continued contritely, "I was out of line. If the rumors floating around the halls are true, we all better be on our best behaviour."

"I know, I know," Elaine exclaimed. "The rumors! It's unbelievable!"

Gunther Grossman, the school shop teacher, ambled through the door. "Hey, ladies," he said, cheerfully. "So what's unbelievable?"

Student Body

"There's a rumor going around that a body has been found on school property," Magda said.

"A rumor, huh? Well, it's possible." He started scrounging around in the cupboards for his favorite mug.

"What do you mean that's *possible*?" Elaine prodded.

Gunther pursed his lips in concentration. "I'm not exactly sure, but the way Velma was acting this morning was odd." He poured coffee into his cup.

"Odd?" Magda joined the conversation. "How so?"

"Well, I was on my way here when I decided to stop in her office for a friendly chat."

Elaine looked up in surprise. "You wanted a friendly chat with dragon lady?"

"What's wrong with that?" Gunther stopped to pour himself a cup of coffee.

Elaine decided not to answer him, but Magda did.

"Well, she's not at the top of *my* list of people I'd like to have a friendly chat with!"

Gunther picked up his coffee mug. "Magda, you're too hard on the woman," he said. "Velma may not win any awards for being the nicest person in town, but there's no denying she's one hot babe." He grinned broadly.

No one said anything.

"Anyway, we're getting off topic here," he said. "We were talking about the rumors going around the school about a possible 'dead body.'"

"That's right," Magda said. "What do you know—or *think* you know?"

"Okay," Gunther resumed his narrative. "so I was on my way to Velma's office, and that's when I spotted her coming through the doorway with her arm around this kid's shoulder. When she went back inside, I went up to the kid to find out what was going on." He paused to gulp down some coffee while it was still hot.

"And?" Julie pressed him further.

"All the kid said was that the VP had ordered him to keep silent, and then he skipped off down the hall."

Elaine looked puzzled. "I don't get it. What does any of this have to do with a dead body being found on school grounds?"

"That's *exactly* what I was wondering," Gunther said. "So I popped my head inside Velma's doorway and saw she was on the phone. The minute she saw me, she put her hand over the receiver and waved me away. So I left."

"You didn't stick around and ask her questions?" Julie said.

"No. I know Velma, and by the way, she's not as bad as any of you seem to think. Anyway, all the signs indicate that she's in a particularly foul mood today, and if I were you, I'd skip the questions about 'a body.' If it should turn out that the rumors are true, I'm sure we'll all hear about it before the day is out."

Julie frowned. "That's it? You don't have any real facts?"

"Nope." He brought the mug up to his lips, concealing the lower half of his face. "I will say *this* though. Judging by the commotion in the halls, my guess is the police have already arrived, and I assume they will be revealing the identity of the body when they're ready."

"Gunther is right. There's no point in guessing," Julie said with resignation. "We'll find out soon enough."

Just then Elaine remembered something. "Magda was saying earlier that Velma might know."

"Velma might know what?"

A statuesque brunette in her early 40's was standing in the doorway as if she had just materialized out of thin air. For several seconds, no one had realized she was there. And that was exactly the way Velma Vorchek liked it.

When she had taken over the reins at Fairmont following Principal Morris's sudden heart attack last November, she took full advantage of her new authority. Sneaking up on people without their knowledge and catching them off guard had become one of her favorite things. She considered it a perk of the job.

"Well?" she said, her voice dripping with acid. "Just exactly what is it I'm supposed to know?"

An uncomfortable silence settled over the staffroom. Finally, Julie cleared her throat.

"We were discussing the rumor that a body had been found in the vacant field beside the parking lot, and we were wondering if you happened to know who it is."

Velma didn't bother to hide her irritation. "Whether I do or I don't, I'm not at liberty to discuss that information," she said stiffly.

What she wasn't saying was that the police had refused to divulge any details to her until a homicide detective arrived. He was expected within the hour, but Velma decided to keep that information to herself.

"Can you at least tell us if this person was a student here?" Elaine asked. She was interrupted by a warning bell telling people they had ten minutes to get to their next class.

Velma turned on her. "Haven't I made myself clear? That information will be revealed when the police are ready to reveal it." She cast a glance around. "Unless I'm mistaken, the Period 5 bell just rang. Don't you people have somewhere to be?"

Julie and Elaine exited quickly, but Magda took her time in getting out the door. Armand, on the other hand, seemed to waver; nevertheless, he put his cup in the sink and prepared to leave. On his way out, he had to slide past Gunther leaning against the wall beside the doorway.

"Leaving so soon, Tinker Bell?" Gunther grinned at him, but there was no warmth in his smile.

Armand scooted past him without bothering to reply.

He had his reasons.

First, and perhaps foremost, Armand's sense of aesthetics was put off by Gunther's apelike appearance. To the French teacher who placed a high value on beauty, the shop teacher's body was beastly. The man was so hairy, the backs of his forearms looked like a battlefield of black spiders. That was bad enough, but then there were Gunther's teeth—small razor sharp incisors which flashed like fangs every time he opened his mouth. However, what really repelled Armand was Gunther's protruding lower jaw. The thing jutted out aggressively as if aiming to take a vicious bite out of anyone who came too close.

Armand kept his distance.

And he wasn't the only one. Whether they voiced their opinions or not, many on staff avoided the shop teacher if they could. On the other hand, there were those who admired Gunther's take-no-prisoners attitude. Of course, his crudeness could be off-putting at times, but his fans were loyal. Among them was Velma Vorchek. Thanks largely to Gunther's excellent coaching skills, she could boast that, for the fifth year running, the school's football team had reached the provincial championship, enhancing Fairmont's reputation in universities across the province. And, as far as

Gunther was concerned, his lack of popularity with some of his peers was their problem, not his.

"Alone at last!" Gunther smirked at the VP scanning notices on the bulletin board.

Velma wheeled around. She was just about to speak when there was a knock on the door. Damn! It had to be for her. It was always for her! With Principal Morris out of commission, the number of problems she was having to deal with had increased significantly, and she was starting to find it tedious.

All she had wanted when she went to the small staff room was a moment's peace and a quick cup of coffee before going back to her busy office which, incredibly, was now crawling with cops.

A dead body on school property! she thought bitterly. *What the hell next?*

Opening the door, Velma found herself face-to-face with an unprepossessing bear of a man in shapeless black slacks and a wrinkled wind breaker. He looked like he could have been one of the school's caretakers, but there was something authoritative in his manner.

"Yes," she said, "may I help you?"

Without waiting for an invitation, the man stepped inside and got right to the point. "I'm Staff Inspector Mike Watts," he said. "Where can I find a Ms. Vorchek?"

"You're the fuzz!" Gunther blurted out.

"Not my *official* title," Watts quipped, turning to address the tall imposing looking woman glaring at him with disapproval. "Can I assume you are Mrs. Vorchek?"

"Yes, I'm Vice Principal Vorchek." Her tone was polite but officious. "Let's go to my office, Inspector, where we can speak privately."

"After you," he said, holding the door for her.

Gunther watched the two of them leave in thoughtful silence. He checked his watch—five minutes until his wood carving class—just enough time to spruce up. Maybe give his breath a spray, slick back his hair—splash some aftershave on his face.

CHAPTER 6
A CASE OF MURDER

12:05 p.m.

Mike Watts followed Velma into her private office and began speaking in a decisive tone of voice.

"I've spoken to my officers who confirmed the presence of a body in the field beside the parking lot, and I've taken a statement from the student who reported the sighting. Now, Ms. Vorchek," he said, "the next order of business is to shut down the school. Students are to be sent home immediately, and teachers need to remain on the premises for questioning." When she didn't budge from behind her desk, he added evenly, "that's an official order, Ms. Vorchek."

She stared hard at him. "Shut down the school?" She seemed more angry than shocked. "And why should I do that?"

"Because we need a clear field in order to conduct our investigation."

She gave the matter some consideration before responding. "I suppose some sort of investigation is necessary; however, you do understand that the body in question could very well belong to one of the homeless people who frequent the neighborhood. Maybe this is someone who got caught in the snowstorm and became disoriented. Or maybe some stoner from one of the crack houses up the street staggered onto the field and decided to lie down in the snow because he was out of his head. That wouldn't be so unusual. Every once in a while one of them wanders onto school property, and we have to deal with it, but we have never, and I mean *never*, closed down the school."

"This neighborhood is not unknown to the police, Ms. Vorchek," the inspector said patiently. "However, when a body is found anywhere in our jurisdiction, the Homicide Squad takes it very seriously."

"Homicide?" She blanched. "You mean he didn't die of an overdose, or an accident, or...?"

"No."

"How do you know?"

"I know, Ms. Vorchek, *I know*."

She sighed deeply. "Wait here." She pushed her chair back and started walking towards the door into the outer office.

From where he was sitting, he could hear Velma's voice over the intercom. "An unexpected development has occurred this morning, and in a few minutes a bell will ring dismissing all students for the rest of the day. Regular classes will resume tomorrow unless otherwise notified via the media by 6 a.m. tomorrow morning. When the bell rings, you are to proceed in an orderly manner to the front doors and exit as quickly as possible. Staff will remain in school to await further instructions."

"Satisfied?" she asked crisply upon returning to her office.

Seconds later the ringing of the bell sent the student body scrambling.

Velma was worried. This wasn't what she had expected when a student came into her office to report on what he had seen on his way to school. She wasn't sure she should believe him. It might have been a hoax—kids playing a game to see what kind of reaction they could get from the school's vice-principal. And with the blinding snowstorm, she wasn't about to tramp out into the field to check it out for herself. That was what the police were for.

So she'd made a decision.

If it was a prank, or if the kid had been mistaken about what he thought he saw—well, no harm done. But if there really was a body on school property, then she would have done the right thing by calling in the proper authorities. She'd had to consider protocol, had to consider consequences. She'd had to cover her ass.

Velma wasn't the only one sizing up the situation. Watts had been quietly observing the person sitting on the other side of the desk. He assessed her coolly.

"So, what now, Inspector?" She gave him a defiant look.

"I'll need a place from which to conduct my interrogations."

Velma thought for a moment. "Okay. You can use Principal Morris's office. The man's on sick leave."

He nodded.

Her voice took on an edge. "How long are your people going to be here? Their presence is very disruptive."

Mike Watts spoke plainly. "Certainly for the rest of the day, Ms. Vorchek."

She found his answer less than satisfying. "Look, Inspector, I need a time frame for when we can get back to normal—particularly if the shutdown extends into tomorrow."

Velma Vorchek was growing increasingly uncomfortable. Minute by minute she had felt control slipping from her grasp. And she didn't like it. She didn't like it one bit.

The inspector had some sense of where she stood. He knew what it was like to be the person shouldering responsibility for the success of a large organization. He was about to convey some compassion when she suddenly lit into him.

"I've done nothing but accommodate you," she began in a tone meant to convey authority as well as annoyance. "I've closed the school and am sending the students home. I'm offering the complete cooperation of my staff," she said, hardly pausing for breath. "When the school does reopen, what do you think will happen when hundreds of kids start swarming the grounds? Do you honestly believe you can keep them from snooping around the parking lot? Well, do you?!"

He took a deep breath. It was a trick he had learned in an anger management seminar he once took as part of his preparation for promotion. He found the course came in handy whenever he had to deal with petty politicians, pretentious oafs, and garden-variety assholes in general.

"Ms. Vorchek," Watts began, measuring his words carefully, "my men have cordoned off the alleged crime scene which will remain so for the next few days. As for a time frame, I cannot be precise, but I would guess we will be here for the better part of the week."

Velma rose abruptly, the legs of her chair scraping across the floor. "A week! I can't shut the school down for a week! I'm responsible to the Board, the parents, and our local trustee. Shutting down the school would create a mountain of problems," she said, shaking with outrage.

"Relax, Ms. Vorchek," Watts said calmly. "School can reopen tomorrow morning as usual. The few detectives who will remain here will be as unobtrusive as possible."

Velma sat back down as the inspector's words slowly sank in. She sighed deeply. "Well, I guess I have no choice in the matter, do I?"

"I'm afraid not."

Student Body

"Okay," she said with resignation. "So what's next on the agenda?"

"We go visit the crime scene."

"*We?*" She looked startled. "Is that necessary?"

"I need verification of the identity of the body—and as quickly as possible."

Velma's face darkened. Suddenly everything took on a different complexion. The media was going to have a field day with this, and that would mean bad publicity for the school—and quite possibly her career.

"You said earlier this was a homicide? Are you absolutely sure?" she asked gravely.

He looked her straight in the eyes. "Yes." He paused. "As Staff Inspector of Metro's Homicide Division, I can assure you that what we have here is a case of murder."

For the first time since the day began, Velma Vorchek felt herself faltering. She stood up a bit shakily and steadied herself by grabbing onto her desk.

"What do you want me to do?" she said simply.

"I'd recommend you put on your coat and boots. The snow is quite deep."

—

Fifteen minutes later the two of them returned to the main office. Together they headed straight for the P.A. system and exchanged a few last minute words before Velma picked up the microphone and began speaking into it in a clear, commanding voice:

"Attention all staff. In exactly ten minutes there will be a meeting for all teachers in the large staff room. Staff Inspector Mike Watts will be speaking about the incident that prompted the police's presence in the school today and the reason for the closure of the school this afternoon."

Ashen faced, she put down the microphone and turned towards him. "Will that do?" she asked weakly.

CHAPTER 7
THE STAFF MEETING

1:30 p.m.

Cautiously teachers made their way among rows of metal chairs lining the larger staffroom. There were occasional murmurs as people filed down rows and found places to sit.

"Please take your seats quickly," Velma ordered from the front of the room. Standing close beside her was Mike Watts. He waited politely as she stepped forward to call the meeting to order.

"You were probably wondering why the police have been on the premises for most of the day," she said. "I called them this morning after I was informed that a body had been spotted in the field next to the teacher parking lot. The police confirmed that fact after their arrival.

"My first thought was that the body belonged to that of a transient from one of the local crack houses or perhaps a homeless person who had stumbled onto school grounds and died in the cold. However, I am sad to inform you that the body has been identified as that of DiAngelo D'Agosta, a student enrolled here at Fairmont."

Gasps were heard throughout the room.

"Let me just stress," Velma continued, "that on the advice of the police, everything said here today must be kept in the strictest confidence. Tomorrow school will resume, and at the end of the day, a letter addressed to parents will be going home with students. For the duration of the investigation and while the police are in the school, I expect the entire staff to cooperate with law enforcement officials so they can do their jobs, and so that we can do ours. And now here to say a few words is the man in charge of the investigation, Staff Inspector Mike Watts of Toronto's Homicide Division."

At the sound of the word 'homicide' a murmur rippled through the room.

—

"Ladies and gentlemen," Inspector Watts began in a strong, steady voice, "what has happened at this school is very serious. A crime has been committed, and the victim's body was left in the vacant field next to the teachers' parking lot. As of this time, we do not know if the victim was killed in the location where he was found, or killed somewhere else and then deposited in the empty field. Our forensic unit should have some answers for us shortly. In the meantime, the crime scene will be cordoned off for the foreseeable future and uniformed officers stationed around its perimeter. It may be necessary for some of you to park your cars on the street for the duration of our investigation.

"As for what you can expect for the remainder of the week—starting tomorrow I will be conducting interviews of the late Mr. D'Agosta's teachers along with those staff members who were in recent contact with the deceased.

"We are also interested in speaking with anyone who knows, or even *thinks* they know, of anything suspicious relating to the death of the late Mr. D'Agosta. If that is you, do not hesitate to speak to me or to one of my men.

"As you exit, you will be handed a card with a number you can call day or night. All calls will be treated with confidentiality.

"Our concern is not only to find the guilty party, but to offer you our protection. It is within the realm of possibility that the killer or killers is still nearby.

"And so, ladies and gentlemen, as you go about your business, keep your eyes and ears open.

"Thank you."

—

Inspector Watts stepped back, and Velma Vorchek took his place. As prearranged, she was ready to make a final announcement before dismissing the meeting. When everyone had settled down, and she had their complete attention, she began.

"There will be no questions taken at this time. We ask that you leave quickly and quietly and take a card with you as you exit the staffroom. Thank you for your patience."

CHAPTER 8
SALAD AND SORROW

5:40 p.m.

The long miserable day was over, and Julie sat at the Formica table in her tiny kitchenette, holding her head in her hands. She hadn't eaten a thing all day, but her mind wasn't on food. Instead, she was thinking about a boy who had scared the hell out of her and then ended up dead.

Looking back on the pre-dawn incident, she felt a sense of relief that she hadn't told anyone yet about the incident in her portable. It didn't take a genius to recognize that divulging that kind of information could easily cast suspicion on her—particularly after she heard the Inspector announce that the body found in the field belonged to Dino. And now that the work day had passed, and with it her opportunity to 'come clean,' so to speak, she was doubly anxious. When she thought about her options, she invariably came to the same conclusion. Her wisest course of action was to keep her mouth shut.

But it was hard.

The knowledge of what had happened that morning weighed heavily on her mind. She truly wished she could talk to someone—someone safe. She thought about ringing up her widowed father in Montreal and proceeded to pick up the phone.

She was about to dial when she hesitated. Julie knew her dad would make an awkward attempt at consoling her, but sooner or later, the conversation would drift back to how lonely he was since the loss of his wife—how miserable his life had become without her—and Julie would start to feel as if she were slowly suffocating. She tried not to blame him, she missed her mother too. But it did occur to her that when her mom passed away, Julie didn't lose one parent, she lost two.

So that only left her ex-boyfriend who had moved out of the flat they shared the day before Labor Day. She had begged him for weeks to move out, but each time he resisted. Finally, to persuade him to leave, she made the case that a first-year teacher was way too busy for a relationship, and in a way, she was right, but that wasn't the real reason. It was just a ruse, and they both knew it.

They had met the year before at the faculty where they shared some of the same classes. Occasionally they went for coffee together. It soon became apparent he was in love with her, but she, on the other hand, wasn't sure of how she felt.

She thought that her ambivalence might be a sign that he really wasn't the right man for her although he was convinced otherwise and had proposed marriage on more than one occasion. Her answer was always no. She didn't even have to think about it.

Finally he came up with a plan he thought would work. He pointed out that, if they shared a flat as roommates, with no strings attached, it would be cost effective, and she would have the option of terminating the arrangement any time she wanted. He was secretly hoping that in the meantime he could convince her that she was actually in love with him and that they were destined to be together. He was wrong.

Certainly the relationship had practical benefits for Julie, but ultimately she came to the realization that, to the outside world, they looked like a real couple. When he filled out their income tax forms and wrote down that they were married, albeit by common law, she was shocked. This wasn't the life she had imagined for herself. This was a lie! A horrible, horrible lie!

From that point on, she spent her days looking for a way out of the maze she had unwittingly walked into.

And then came graduation from the Faculty of Education and with it teaching credentials and a door to the future. *Her* future.

She approached him with an ultimatum. Either he moved out or she would. It wasn't fair, she said, to either one of them to continue with what was, essentially, a mockery of marriage.

He complied, albeit reluctantly, and offered to remain friends. And now that she really needed a friend, she was tempted to call him, but just like with her father, she hesitated. Her instinct told her he would seize the opportunity to try to weasel his way back into her life, and in her vulnerable state, she just couldn't risk it.

Comfort, it seemed, came at a cost. A cost she was no longer willing to pay. So, for the present, the two men in her life would have to be Ben and Jerry.

Julie dug out a big spoon from the silverware drawer and loaded it up with Rocky Road. As the cool sweetness of the ice cream melted on her tongue, her mind began to go backwards, reliving events of the past several hours.

It had been a *Macbeth* sort of day—sad and dreary. And shockingly violent as well. A boy was dead. A crazy, mixed-up, impossible boy who would now never become a man. She shook her head and wondered woefully if maybe that wasn't a good thing. The world didn't need another sexual predator. And if she hadn't had the wit to stay calm, and if the snow globe hadn't been within easy reach—who knows what might have happened. She shuddered at the thought.

Julie got up and put the ice cream back in the freezer. Some part of her recognized that she was feeding the little girl inside her. If she was going to live in an adult world, she had to eat like one. She could hear her mother saying those very words when Julie had been a child living at home in Montreal. Thinking about her French-Canadian mother brought a smile to her lips for the first time that day.

"Okay, Ma, I'll make a big nutritious salad—just for you," she said out loud, as if saying the words would make the past become the present and the present become bearable. "Just for you…"

She dragged herself around her tiny kitchenette gathering a collection of chickpeas and kidney beans from the cupboard and cherry tomatoes and green onions from the fridge. Finally she sat down in front of a big bowl of bean salad glistening with olive oil. She sighed. The day was over, the die was cast, and there was not one thing she could do about it.

Not one blessed thing.

CHAPTER 9
PEROGIES AND PAIN

5:45 p.m.

After the impromptu staff meeting had mercifully ended, Magda spent a few hours in her classroom fine tuning the lineup of courses for the coming weeks. She then decided she would walk home rather than call for a taxi as her mother had suggested when she dropped her off that morning. The snow had stopped, and Magda knew the sidewalks would be cleared by now, so she could get a good footing—especially with her walking stick for support.

However, only a few minutes into her trip home, her knees were already telling her that she should have followed her mother's advice. Her arthritis—a legacy handed down through several generations—was making walking difficult. In her youth, she had been a powerhouse athlete, but, alas, those days were long gone.

It would be a *long* walk home.

Student Body

—

Shedding her coat, Magda quietly entered the living room where her father was snoring peacefully in his leather Barcalounger. A note folded in half and propped up like a tent was waiting for her on the coffee table. It said her mother was at church and wouldn't be home until late, but that there was a casserole of perogies being kept warm in the oven and some cold poached salmon in the fridge. A postscript informed her that tomorrow would be baking day and everyone could look forward to her famous apricot strudel, so "not to worry."

Magda smiled with bemusement. Strong coffee and hot strudel. These were the cures for everything that was wrong with the world, or so her mother was convinced. And who knew, Magda shrugged, maybe the woman was right.

Popping a few 222s into her mouth, she plopped down in a chair at the kitchen table and poured herself an ice-cold glass of Chardonnay. With her background in science, she knew it wasn't wise to mix drugs with alcohol, but at that moment, she simply didn't care. Her day had been very stressful, pure and simple. Sometimes you had to break a few rules.

Magda loaded up her plate and ate heartily. She finished her dinner by brewing a fresh cup of coffee which she stealthily carried past her sleeping father and up to her room. Once she had donned her dressing gown and settled back against the pillows on her bed, then—and only then—did she allow her mind to dwell on the one subject she had been studiously avoiding for hours:

DiAngelo D'Agosta.

—

It was the end of November, the day before Term Two officially began, and teachers were scurrying about like frantic ants. There were textbooks to be counted, class lists to be located, and photocopier codes to be confirmed. No one was idle.

To everyone's relief, it happened to be a free day for the kids, so teachers and guidance counselors could get ready for the onslaught the following day. Most kids had already preregistered, but there were always last minute exceptions.

The halls were relatively empty except for a few ambitious students who could be found here and there, seeking to satisfy their curiosity about the upcoming term. One of those nosing about was a tall, dark-haired boy by the name of DiAngelo D'Agosta.

As department head, Magda was in her classroom going over the roster for the science courses and checking out requests for teaching assignments. She wanted to accommodate everyone, if at all possible, but it was a challenging job. She had been concentrating so hard that she failed to notice the boy leaning against her doorway, hands in his pockets, a rakish grin on his handsome face.

Student Body

When he still had not been acknowledged, Dino casually strolled up to her desk and stood directly in front of it. It was a bold bid for attention, and Magda was intrigued. She liked a show of confidence so long as it did not verge on cockiness. She raised her head but did not smile.

"Yes, young man," she said, her eyes taking in one of the most beautiful human beings she had ever seen. Maybe, Magda thought, that was where his confidence came from. Attractive people can often be spoiled. Anyone who reads the tabloids knows that. In any case, she found the boy interesting. "What can I do for you?"

Dino took his time before answering. He had already figured out that life was a lot like playing poker. To get what you wanted, first you studied your hand, then you sized up your opponents. The game required one to be both crafty and cool, and Dino knew he was very good at being both. Occasionally he had run into a little resistance, but this dough faced, frumpy science teacher was hardly a challenge. He figured the woman had to be over forty and probably a virgin. She was obviously a sex-starved middle-aged female just ripe for the kind of subtle seduction he had perfected to a fine art.

"Ms. Malinsky," he said, speaking to her as if they were old friends, "my name is Dino D'Agosta, and I just found out you're the top dog in this department." He paused to give her a playful wink. "So I was wondering if you wouldn't mind giving me some advice."

Magda put down her pen and fixed him with a level gaze. "Advice? What kind of advice?"

"Well, I'm going to university in the fall, and I need a science credit," he said sliding around her desk until he was standing right beside her. Then, before she could react, he jumped up and plunked himself down on her desktop. Magda was slightly taken aback by his audacity but decided she would wait to see what his next move would be. This kid was putting on one hell of a show.

"So, as I was saying," he purred, "I think physics would be too hard for me, and frankly, chemistry sounds boring. That only leaves biology and *you*. So what do you say? I know it's past the deadline, but can I get into your biology class?"

"The quota has been filled," she replied. "You can wait until the spring term. Or you take it in summer school."

Unimpressed with her answer, Dino decided it was time to up the ante. "Do you mean to tell me you can't squeeze in just one more *really* grateful student? Give a guy a break?" His big brown eyes took on the pleading look of a lost puppy. Magda remained impassive.

Encouraged by her silence, Dino reached over and gently smoothed down the hair on one side of her face, running his hand lightly over her ear in a provocative manner.

Now he had crossed a line. In all her years of teaching, no student had ever dared to touch her in such an intimate fashion. "What do you think you're doing!?" she demanded.

Student Body

"Just showing you some of the advantages of saying 'yes.'" He smiled slyly.

Magda took a second to consider before responding. "So," she said in an even voice, "if I admit you to the class, what exactly can I expect?"

Dino straightened his shoulders. This was going to be much easier than he had imagined. "Well, for starters, we could experiment with some exploratory touching in the broom closet during the lunch break. And after that, we might proceed to the next step in a motel of your choosing. Not to brag, of course," he said, seductively, "but I really know how to start a fire in a woman's heart."

He leaned in a little closer. Dino felt like laughing. No one knew how to play the game better than he did. No one.

"So," he said, after giving her a minute to think it over, "how does that sound?"

Magda shifted in her chair, twisting her body sideways until she was directly facing him.

"Okay," she said, giving him one of her brightest smiles. "That's what I can expect from you. Now would you like to know what you can expect from me?"

"Yes, please." Dino was salivating. His science credit was in the bag.

"Well," she said, using the tip of her forefinger to softly stroke the fleshy region between his upper lip and the bottom of his nose. "I can ram the ball of my hand against this particular spot with the force of sledgehammer, and you would be dead in seconds. It's a move I learned during my university days when I was a Black Belt," she said cheerily. "Of course, I have a few other tricks up my sleeve, but I think that one has your name written on it."

Dino's face went white. He started backing up.

"You're some kind of bitch, you know that?" He spat the words out with disgust.

"And you, young man, are some kind of bastard."

Dino stopped at the door and stared contemptuously at the science teacher who excelled at giving lessons. "I have friends in high places," he sneered. "Suppose I tell one of them what you just said. How long do you think you would keep your job?"

"Long enough to dispense with you," she said sagely. "Oh, and one more thing, you mess with anyone on staff—and I mean *anyone*— and the person you're going to be dealing with is me."

"Is that a threat?"

"Of *course* it is," she smiled sweetly and went back to sorting out her course lists.

CHAPTER 10
TOURTIERE AND TEMPTATION

Armand studied his liquor cabinet with abstract concentration. He needed a drink—something sweet and soothing to soften the sharp edges of this interminable day. Perhaps a glass of sherry. Yes, that might do.

Lovingly he carried his drink over to his ergonomic Scandinavian lounger situated at just the right angle to take advantage of the view of the Toronto Islands outside his floor-to-ceiling window. True, it had cost him a pretty penny to get a unit on the twentieth floor in his waterfront condominium, but it was worth it. There wasn't a doubt in his mind.

On his way home from school, he had taken a slight detour to the Summerhill Market located in Rosedale, an upscale area of the city. The deli was a bit out of the way, but no shop this side of Montreal made a more authentic Quebec-Style tourtiere with a to-die-for flaky crust. At that moment, the delicious pork pie was sitting on his marble kitchen countertop, just waiting to be reheated in the oven and then served up on Armand's finest Wedgewood china. Of course, he knew a well-balanced meal required some source of vegetables, but he was too tired to even think about all the preparation required, so a bag of raw baby carrots would have to suffice for what could be classified as roughage.

As hungry as he was, however, Armand found he couldn't stir himself to get up off his lounger. Instead, he stared blindly at the kaleidoscope of colors on a night-crossing ferry taking commuters to their cottage homes in the fading glow of twilight. How he longed to relax—to put the events of the day out of his mind—but he found it impossible. It was like having a sore tooth that your tongue can't stop probing as if compelled by some invisible force to seek out the very thing that is causing such torment.

He leaned back and closed his eyes. A memory was tugging at his brain like an obnoxious two-year-old who wouldn't leave him alone.

When was it? Late last October? Early November? He wasn't sure. He did remember that the day had been brisk with a light coating of frost covering the ground, and all he had wanted when he arrived for work that morning was to get out of his car and hustle to the warmth of the main building without delay.

Leaning back on his lounger, Armand took several sips of his sherry. Soon he closed his eyes and his mind began to drift back to a day not that long ago…

—

Student Body

He had been hastening across the teacher parking lot when he spotted two figures huddled in the shadows of the shop portable. He decided to stop and take a closer look. When he did, he couldn't believe his eyes. A girl was kneeling on the frozen ground in front of a boy who was leaning back against the portable wall. Her thin coat had been thrown around her shoulders to act as a cloak shielding her from prying eyes.

Armand thought she looked young enough to have been a student at Fairmont, but it was impossible to tell. Her face was obscured from view. However, the girl's identity seemed to be a matter of indifference to the boy standing in front of her with his hands grasping either side of her head, holding it in place like a vise.

Armand was speechless. He stared hard at the boy whose distinct features were now recognizable in the deepening dawn. It was definitely one of his students—the boy known around school as the Italian Stallion.

Armand cleared his throat loudly to announce his presence. Startled, the girl stumbled to her feet and started running towards the anonymity of the street until the semi-darkness swallowed her whole. Dino, on the other hand, merely shrugged and smiled sheepishly like a kid who had been caught with his hand in the cookie jar.

It was the gall of the boy more than anything that raised Armand's hackles. Dino's notorious reputation was known to all the staff at Fairmont High, but Armand did expect the boy to be at least contrite, if not embarrassed. Dino was neither.

"What's the matter, teach," he asked lightly, shoving his shirt tail down into his pants. "Not getting your share?"

The effrontery of this kid was beyond bearing. "I think you better pull yourself together, young man, and come with me. I'm sure Principal Morris would like to hear about this."

Dino paused, seemingly in thought. "Is that really necessary?" he said, tugging at his zipper. "Why don't we go to your classroom and talk about it?"

Armand's eyes widened. "Well, it is cold out here," he said, nervously casting a quick look around.

"I'm sure it's warmer in your car." Dino's voice was like velvet. "And, if it isn't, I know how to heat things up."

"I have to be in class in half an hour," Armand stammered. That damn boy! He was so beautiful! That damn, damn boy!

"Half an hour?" Dino started strolling towards the French teacher in long leisurely strides. "That's three times as long as I need," he grinned wickedly.

Armand started to shiver and not just from the cold. His career was at stake—he had to be crazy to even consider this boy's proposition.

"Listen, kid," he began, struggling for words, "this kind of thing could get me fired."

Student Body

"Only if someone talks." By now Dino had reached Armand's side. "Look at it this way, teach," he said with a reassuring smile, "it's a sweet deal. You'll have the goods on me, and I'll have the goods on you. I think that's what's called *quid pro quo*—just a little something I learned in civics class last year." He arched his eyebrows in amusement.

"Okay, but we have to be discreet."

Dino laughed. "My thoughts exactly."

CHAPTER 11
RAVIOLI AND REGRETS

6:30 p.m.

Elaine Richardson was tired—more tired than she remembered being in a long time. The staff meeting had taken a lot out of her, and she was starting to wonder if maybe she should give up teaching after all and go for early retirement. There was so much of the world she hadn't seen. Polynesia. Pompeii. The Great Wall of China. Some of her couple friends had tried to persuade her to go on exotic trips with them, but that was when her husband was still alive, and she had to politely decline. The man just wasn't into travelling. He liked his creature comforts too much to spend hours waiting in airport terminals or come home incapacitated by mind blowing diarrhea, courtesy of some nasty tropical bug.

So, in the end Elaine stayed put—in her house, in her job and, most importantly, in her marriage. And the fact was she didn't really mind. Life can be most pleasant when one knows what to expect from day-to-day. It might get a

Student Body

little dull now and then, but that was a small price to pay for safety.

Safety.

Elaine shuddered at the word. It was something she had taken for granted for so long that she forgot what it felt like *not* to be safe. And then, one day, she had thrown safety away. Just casually thrown it away, as if being safe was nothing more than a matter of convenience—a simple little non-essential one could take or leave, like a pack of gum stored in the bottom of one's purse.

Elaine trotted wearily to the kitchen. It was time to microwave leftovers from the night before when her married son had come for a visit with his wife and daughter. Elaine had pulled out all the stops for the occasion, making a lavish Italian dinner with gobs and gobs of mozzarella. Her little granddaughter was into pasta in a big way, and the girl was crazy about gooey cheese.

And it had been fun!

She hadn't cooked a full meal since she couldn't remember when. What was the point? Why fill the refrigerator with leftovers that would spoil before she could get around to finishing them? There was a time when Elaine took pride in creating gourmet meals for her family, but after the kids left and her husband died, the house was empty. Sooner than she expected, she began to think of dinner as something to get through as efficiently and as quickly as possible.

But tonight was different. Tonight she wasn't in a hurry. Tonight she was going to enjoy her meal and then linger over a glass of Bordeaux. And when she had eaten the remnants of last night's ravioli and loaded the dishwasher, she was going to sit back in her leather recliner and reflect on the day she had just been through—a day that was rapidly receding into a past that refused to die, unlike the boy whose body had been found in the vacant lot that morning.

The boy for whom she had thrown safety away.

—

Three weeks earlier…

"You have a beautiful home."

Dino stood in the middle of Elaine's intricate East Indian rug, glancing around her living room. It was a Saturday, one week before Christmas Break, and he had come at Elaine's invitation for some last-minute tutoring.

"I've never seen a sofa this color before," he smiled, lowering himself onto her turquoise couch cushions. "It's quite exquisite."

"It was my late husband's idea," Elaine called from the kitchen. "He said leather furniture eliminated the potential for germs. The man had an absolute obsession about cleanliness, probably from having to wash his hands so often as a surgeon."

Student Body

She poured chocolate syrup into two mugs of hot milk and began stirring each one. She stared at the swirling liquid in each cup as if transfixed. *Oh, why not?* she thought, answering the question in her mind. *It isn't a school day.*

She reached into the tall cupboard for her bottle of Baileys Irish Cream. She meant to pour a small amount into her hot chocolate but the liqueur came out too fast, and she ended up with much more in her cup than she had intended. Warily she took a sip. It was delicious, if a bit strong. Then, picking up the tray holding the two mugs of hot chocolate, she headed into the living room.

Carefully she set the frothy drinks down on the coffee table in front of her young guest and handed him his cup. "Please choose one of the wooden coasters to put under your cup. They're all unique," she said proudly. "My late husband made them many years ago when he was an intern at Toronto Western. At the time his hobby was wood carving. He said it was relaxing, but then he got so busy with his practice, he had to give it up. I believe his tools are still around here somewhere."

She joined Dino on the sofa. "The one you're holding now is particularly special," she said, sipping her hot chocolate. "It was made from a piece of wood that was once part of a magnificent maple in front of our home on Humberview Road near the Old Mill subway station. The whole area was full of stately trees, and ours was one of the most majestic in the neighborhood. Unfortunately, it was so severely damaged in an ice storm several years ago we had to have it cut down." She paused to take a large sip of cocoa which had cooled considerably.

Dino turned the coaster over in his hand, then held it up to his eyes. "It looks like there's some kind of dog on one side and what appears to be the letter 'R' on the other," he said uncertainly.

"You're quite correct," Elaine agreed, downing the rest of her hot chocolate. "There's an 'R' for Richardson carved on the back of each coaster, and on the front are different types of terriers."

He peered at what was obviously the shape of a dog. "I'm afraid I don't recognize it." He turned towards her, an inquiring look on his handsome face.

"It's a Dandie Dinmont," she said, her eyes sparkling. "That little coaster is so much more than just another one of my husband's wood carvings." Feeling a little light headed, she paused to collect her thoughts before continuing. "I know it's corny to say, but it's actually a little piece of my heart. You see, many years ago when the two of us were first married, we had a little dog just like the one on the coaster you're holding. Her name was Dinah, and the three of us were as close as any family could be." She sighed. "Of course, there are photos galore of those days, but this little bit of wood created from the corpse of a tree in our front yard is irreplaceable." Her eyes were starting to mist. "It's a tangible symbol of a time when I was a young wife living with a great guy and a wonderful dog. Nothing on earth would ever make me part with it," she said with a catch in her throat.

Dino sat quietly watching her as Elaine continued to stare at the small round wooden object that obviously meant so much to her. Then, without warning, she began to crumble before his eyes, her composure collapsing as the force of her emotions swept over her like a tsunami. She couldn't stop sobbing.

Dino put his arms around her and held her closely.

"It's all right," he spoke soothingly, as if to a hurt child. "Loss is a painful thing. Go ahead and cry. It's all right. Cry for as long as you like. I'm here for you." He started massaging her shaking shoulders until at last she buried her head in his chest.

―

When Elaine woke up, she instinctively stretched out an arm for the alarm clock on the nightstand beside her bed. What she saw was startling. Something like an hour had gone by, and she couldn't account for the time!

Hastily she propped herself up on her elbows. From across the room, Dino was comfortably ensconced in one of the bedroom accent chairs next to Elaine's mahogany bureau. He seemed to be studying her.

Suddenly she felt afraid. This was wrong! All wrong! How did she go from having a cup of cocoa in the living room to this?! Had she lost her mind?

At least, she realized with some relief, she was still wearing the clothes she had on when the boy showed up at her house hours earlier. That was something, anyway.

"What happened?" she asked, still a bit groggy but sobering up fast. "The last I remember we were sitting on the couch, talking."

"Nothing happened," Dino said, giving her a friendly smile. "You were upset, and I carried you in here and deposited you on your bed," he explained patiently. "You were so exhausted from crying, you fell asleep."

It sounded plausible. And yet it didn't. Elaine was confused, but one thing was clear. She had to get this boy out of her house—stat!

"I'm sorry about that," she said, thinking quickly. "We'll have a tutoring session one day after school soon—in study hall—but right now I want you to leave." She stared hard at him. For the first time, she realized how foolish she had been to allow this kid to come into her home. If he refused to go, then what?

"Okay," Dino said, jumping up from the chair. "Do you mind if I call you tonight? Just to make sure you're all right?" he said heading out of her bedroom while she followed him to the front door.

"I'm perfectly fine. You don't have to call."

"I think I will anyway," he said, leaning down to kiss her lightly on the forehead. Then he picked up his things and left.

—

"Hi, it's Dino," the voice on the phone announced.

"I told you not to call," Elaine responded calmly. Actually she was anything but calm. Something told her she was in way over her head.

"Well, I wanted to tell you how much I appreciated hearing that story about the coaster and your little dog."

Elaine was at a loss. This kid wanted something. But what?

"Yes." It was all she could think of to say.

"I liked it so much, I decided to slip the coaster into my backpack so I could show it to Velma and share your story with her. She'd get a kick out it."

"WHAT?!"

"Of course, I don't really have to do that. I'm willing to make a trade, and I'll keep my mouth shut in the bargain."

Elaine closed her eyes and leaned against the wall. "Trade for what?" she said tightly.

"An 'A' on the mid-terms."

"Are you crazy?!"

"Here's how it's going to play out," he said coolly. Elaine could almost see the smirk on his face as he dictated his demands. "You hand back my test paper with an 'A' on it, and I'll hand you the coaster. Oh, and neither of us will discuss this with Velma."

This was a nightmare. It had to be!

"You call the Vice-Principal by her first name?" Elaine's voice was flat, lifeless.

"Of course. We're friends." Dino had to suppress a laugh. It was all going so well!

"And if I refuse?"

"You'll never get your precious coaster back… or your reputation. Think it over."

CHAPTER 12
PIZZA AND PROMISES

6:45 p.m.

Gunther lay on his back in his king size bed with his arms folded beneath his head. His mood was as black as the ugly bruise under his fingernail—a reminder that accidents can happen in shop class, even to a teacher with 26 years of experience in handling dangerous tools.

What a fucking day it had been! If it were possible, he would like to smash the entire day to bits with one of the brass head carving mallets he kept stored in his classroom. That's what this day deserved.

Gunther groaned and turned on his side. The ache in his stomach forced him to think about food. He didn't know what he wanted to eat, he just knew he wanted *something*. He closed his eyes and focused on the things he liked best—jalapeno peppers, spicy Italian sausage, smoky Provolone. *Eureka!* He reached for the phone. A giant pizza and a couple of cold Molsons were just what he needed to get out of this funk.

He placed the call and grabbed a beer from the fridge. Then he found a fancy placemat that had once been part of a wedding present. He had married late in life. It was a bad call. When his ex-wife walked out, she left everything behind, including her contempt.

The bitch said she wasn't into "sharing." Said she was fed up with his never being home at night.

Well, all that was in the past. And, fortunately, it hadn't cost him a cent. All she wanted was a quick divorce and her cat. Gunther was happy to oblige. It had been as easy as ordering pizza.

Gunther smiled to himself when he remembered what he had filled in as 'reason for the separation' on the legal documents. "The woman's a pain in the ass," he had written in big block letters. The look on his lawyer's face when he read it had Gunther doubled over in laughter. "That's a good joke, Gunther," his lawyer said, smiling lightly, "but I'm afraid the judge won't think so. Better change that to irreconcilable differences." And the divorce became a done deal.

Gunther began scrounging around in his catch-all drawer for a bottle opener, swearing the whole time. It took him a good five minutes to find the damn thing. He had to admit it. His kitchen was a monument to messiness. Not even ordered disorder. Just complete chaos. Gunther grunted and slammed the drawer shut.

So, he wasn't into housekeeping. Big deal! He had a full-time job, for god's sake. And a demanding diva for a boss. Of course, she more than made up for that with legs from here to Sunday and a tush so firm you could crack an egg on it. Those were definite assets, he smiled to himself. And, lucky for him, those feelings were reciprocated. In the future, he might need the kind of influence a person in Velma's position could provide. Yes, he was a lucky man indeed.

—

Dinner was over and Gunther dutifully filled the sink with the dirty dishes, then turned on the tap full blast before squirting Palmolive into the oily mix. It was time to head for bed.

He was beyond exhausted and wanted nothing more than to drop off to sleep, but when he flopped onto his mattress, his mind kept returning to the news of the day. Dino D'Agosta was found dead in the field next to the teachers' parking lot.

—

If only Gunther could get some sleep. He thought about loading up on prescription sleeping pills and washing the whole thing down with a shot of whiskey. The question was would that be enough to block out images of the most beautiful boy this side of heaven—or hell, as the case may be.

There were so many memories churning around inside Gunther's head, it felt like a spinning dryer. Some were sweet, like the time he mentioned to his wood carving class he was having trouble sleeping at night, and a voice from the back of the room yelled out, "Just jerk off." Everybody laughed, including Gunther. "Thanks, Dino," he grinned. That kid was something else.

Then there was the time he asked the boy to stay after class to discuss his many absences. "If you don't start coming to class," Gunther warned, "I'll have to drop you from the course."

"Oh?" he sneered. "How would that look—I mean after you were so nice to me—taking me to a hockey game and all," he smiled snidely. "People might start to wonder …"

"You ungrateful punk. I was just trying to help you after hearing about your rotten home life. And you pay me back by being late or skipping class altogether? That's going to end right now," he said. "Either you start attending class—and on time—or I *will* kick you out of the course."

"Throw me out of *shop class*?! A 'frill' course! And that's supposed to hurt me? How?" Dino snickered.

Gunther took a deep breath. "Every course is important. And attendance, or lack thereof, will show up on your transcript—that is, assuming you graduate from high school." It was about as polite as the shop teacher was willing to be with this insufferable smart-ass.

"I don't believe you are correct, Gunther." Dino looked steadily into his teacher's eyes. "You just made that up to keep me in class." He draped an arm over his teacher's shoulder as if to console him.

Gunther shrugged off Dino's arm. "It's *Mr.* Grossman to you, kid. And I couldn't care less whether you show up or not. Skip class all you want. It's your funeral."

"*Really?* You wouldn't miss seeing my ass every day?" Dino eyes were laughing.

Gunther was livid. At that moment, all he wanted out of life was to punch this punk in the mouth until that beautiful face was nothing more than a mask—a wet, sticky, oozing mask dripping blood on the shop room floor.

"Listen, you little shit," Gunther spoke between clenched teeth. "I don't want you to come back to my class. Now get lost, and if I see you again, you'll find out exactly how creative I can be with a woodcarving tool."

—

Gunther dragged himself out of bed, picked up his bottle off the floor, and schlepped his way to the medicine cabinet. No matter what happens in the morning, he told himself as he filled a bathroom Dixie cup with whiskey, tonight he would get some rest.

CHAPTER 13
SCALLOPS AND SCANDAL

7:00 p.m.

Velma had stayed at school for hours after the staff meeting. It was now close to 7:00 pm, and she debated what she should do—keep plugging away at paperwork or go home to an empty house? *Not much of a choice.* She climbed into her coat.

The drive home was uneventful thanks to the steady work of the city snowplows. As she stood in her doorway, she found she was too tired to even take off her coat. Instead she allowed it to slip off her shoulders and slide onto the floor. Then she turned and hung her keys on the hook above the bench where she usually sat to pull on her boots. She wouldn't even have bothered doing that much except for the memory of a frantic morning last fall when her entire world came to a halt while she tore the house apart searching for those missing keys. Now she never failed to replace them as soon as she walked through the door.

Having shed her coat and removed her boots, she moved further into the room and sank into the comfortable cushions of her easy chair. Finally she propped her feet up on the leather ottoman and closed her eyes.

Velma made a concerted effort to forget everything that had happened that day. Only it wasn't working. She simply couldn't relax. Her mind was a storm, a full blown tornado with cars flying through plate glass windows and two-storey houses smashing into trucks on the highway. Everything was bedlam—her thoughts, her life, her world.

Maybe some dinner would help calm her nerves. She hadn't eaten a thing since breakfast several hours ago. She tried to remember what was in the refrigerator, but it was no use. She couldn't handle food right now. Her gut was too full of rage.

Men! She was heartily sick of them!

First, there was her sorry excuse of a husband who had decided, after fourteen years of marriage, that what he really needed was a new life, preferably with a new woman. And he had one already picked out—a perky little 23-year-old who waited tables at the Swiss Chalet where he and Velma used to dine the occasional Friday night. Oh, yes, she was *the One*. Definitely.

Then there were the classic examples of manhood at her workplace, Armand and Gunther—one a dilettante, the other a degenerate—although if she were honest with herself, she did consider Gunther a friend. Sure, he was rough around the edges, but he was amusing, and more importantly, he was good in the sack. Of course, she was the boss, and if she wanted to get rid of any of them, it wouldn't be that difficult. For months, she had had a source who supplied her with useful information, should the need arise. Occasionally the thought had crossed her mind that she herself could be incriminated by that very same source.

And then, today—that rumpled caveman of a cop giving her orders, pushing his weight around! He was the one in charge now, not her! And what's more, he was going to be in her face for the entire week!

However, there was another male on her mind at the moment and she couldn't stop thinking about him.

—

Three weeks earlier…

Velma was tapping her toe on her shiny hardwood floor with obvious annoyance. If she was hoping to send a message, it had no effect on the handsome boy stretched out on her sofa, a small throw pillow beneath his curly head.

"So," she asked bluntly, "*why* did your mother throw you out of the house?"

"The usual." Dino yawned, obviously bored. "Her boyfriends were paying more attention to me than to her." He bolted upright. "What's for supper?"

Velma shook her head in amazement. The nerve of this kid! Less than fifteen minutes ago he had shown up on her doorstep with his khaki-colored backpack and walked right in like he owned the place. Then he marched over to her couch, flopped down without bothering to take off his shoes, and now he was demanding dinner!

"You *can't* stay here," she said, her face devoid of any expression. If there had been the slightest trace of welcome in her voice, Dino would have detected it, and she'd be a goner. It wasn't that she was in love with this seventeen-year-old boy; it was something else. Something sick—like a mysterious disease that remains in the body long after the symptoms have disappeared, only to reoccur without warning, time and time again.

"Why not?" Dino seemed sincerely at a loss as to why he, a high school senior, couldn't simply move in with the woman who happened to be the divorced vice-principal at his high school.

Velma thought about trying to explain the concept of propriety to him, but what was the use? In Dino's world, rules were for losers—those sad, pathetic people in the workaday world trudging through life as if it were an obstacle to overcome, an obligation to be endured.

Velma made a decision.

"All right, you can stay—that is, until we find a placement for you in a group home. And understand this," she said in the firmest possible tone. "You're sleeping in the guest room."

"Of course," Dino replied, his eyes sparkling like lights at the midway. "I wouldn't have it any other way... Now, as I was saying—what's for supper?"

"How do you feel about scallops?"

"What is that? Some kind of fish?"

Velma turned her face away so the boy wouldn't see her smile. "It's seafood."

"I don't have a problem with that," Dino said, staring pointedly at her legs. "Pretty good gams for a woman of forty-two." He leered at her.

Velma looked shocked. "How'd you know my age?"

"I know everything about you," he said. "Now, what will you be serving with the scallops?"

"Rice, if you like."

"Is that the best you can do?" he asked archly. "I'm a growing boy."

Slowly he got up from the sofa and started heading in her direction.

Velma froze. She watched warily while Dino began gliding towards her in smooth, seamless strides like a stalking cat. As he got nearer, she started stumbling backwards. Dino caught her just as she was about to fall.

Student Body

—

Well, that was then. Velma sighed. The hour was getting quite late, and she needed to put all of it behind her. Morning would come soon enough, and with it a school reeling from the aftershock of Dino's death.

Drunk with exhaustion, Velma stumbled into her bedroom and collapsed onto her bed. As soon as her head hit the pillow, the last thought that flashed across her mind was of a boy—a boy who was as delightful as he was disturbing. And deeply, deeply dangerous.

TUESDAY

CHAPTER 14
"TYPICAL TEENAGE STUFF."

6:15 a.m.

Watts directed the beam of his flashlight on the cordoned off area where Dino's body had been found. He was well aware that forensics had already scoped out the place on the day of the murder, and it was unlikely that anything of significance had been missed. *Still*, he thought as he swept his flashlight methodically over the area, *a second look couldn't hurt.*

"Find anything?" A young detective on the other side of the yellow tape, was straining to see into the darkness.

"Not yet, Paul."

Watts had specifically chosen this particular police recruit to assist in the investigation and with good reason. Of all the recent graduates from the academy, the 29-year-old was head and shoulders above the rest—in more ways than one.

Student Body

At six five, he got a lot of ribbing from the guys on the force about his name. Paul Bunyan. That didn't faze him. In fact, when the kidding started, he would sometimes swing his arms through the air, pretending to be a lumberjack felling a tree with an imaginary ax. The guys howled.

What the Staff Inspector especially appreciated about the young rookie was the fact that he never lost his cool. The kid was as relaxed as a coon hound soaking up sunshine on a lazy summer day.

"So, what do you think?" Bunyan said.

"What do I think?" Mike answered, straightening up. "The evidence seems to indicate that the victim was ambushed. What puzzles me is where did that second, smaller wound come from?"

"Could there have been more than one assailant?"

"Possible—quite possible." Watts nodded thoughtfully.

"You think maybe the motive was robbery?" Bunyan said. "Some drifter or a drunk staggering home saw an opportunity?"

"I doubt it. The force used to inflict the wound at the back of the skull indicates a crime of passion. This kid had enemies."

"It was personal?"

"I believe so. And my money's on someone who works here."

"A teacher?" Bunyan seemed genuinely surprised.

"Call it a hunch, but I believe that someone on staff was pushed too far."

Just then, headlights appeared at the street entrance to the school's parking lot. A few seconds later a small grey Toyota pulled into an empty spot, and a young woman got out of the car.

It was just after 6:30.

—

"Excuse me, Miss." Bunyan strolled up to the woman taking a school satchel out of the trunk of her car. "I'm Detective Paul Bunyan, and this is Staff Inspector Mike Watts of the Homicide Squad."

Julie Gauvin jumped. "You startled me," she said, trying to catch her breath. "Who did you say you are?"

"Paul Bunyan."

Julie's eyes were starting to adjust to the darkness. She looked at the tall young detective standing over her. "You say your name is Paul Bunyan?"

Bunyan suppressed a smile. "I suppose you're wondering where I keep my blue ox, Babe."

Watts stepped forward. "You're one of the teachers here?"

"Yes, Inspector." Julie turned her attention to the man she recognized from the staff meeting. "I teach English." Then she said, "It's my first year at Fairmont."

She had no idea why she added that bit of information. It couldn't have been relevant. She reproached herself for saying too much. Nervous people always say too much.

"Could you show us your classroom?" Watts asked.

Julie knew it was not a request. "Of course. This way."

She started walking briskly towards her portable. When she unlocked the door, the two men waited for her to enter, then the three of them moved to the front of the room where Julie deposited her school satchel and assorted cleaning supplies on top of her desk.

"What can I do for you gentlemen?" she asked, turning around to face them.

"Is this the time you usually arrive at work?" the inspector asked.

"Yes."

"Doesn't the first class start at 8:15?"

"That's right, but I always come in early to tidy up the place."

"It takes two hours to clean a classroom?"

Julie started fidgeting. "No. I'm usually finished by 6:50 a.m. Then I review my notes for the day."

"Are you alone during that time?" He narrowed his eyes. Something was amiss here, he just didn't know what.

"Yes. That is until 7:45 when students are allowed to come in if they need a place to study."

"So, on the morning of the murder, from approximately 6:30 until 7:45 a.m., you were alone in your classroom. Is that correct?" Watts thought he detected a slight twitch in the young teacher. Bunyan noticed it too.

Julie hesitated. What if someone had seen Dino through the window? What if he ran into someone when he left and told them where he'd been? Should she tell the detectives what had happened that morning? Would that protect her? Or would it put her in greater jeopardy?

Julie knew the men were waiting for her response.

"Yes," she answered thinly. She was sure that they didn't believe her.

A few seconds went by in silence as if both men were expecting her to say more. When she didn't, Bunyan spoke up. "Excuse me, Miss," he said gently. "You seem anxious. Is there something you'd like to tell us?"

She inhaled deeply. "No, not really."

Watts studied her carefully. She was lying. He was sure of it. He decided to let it go—for the moment

"What's your name?" he asked.

"Julie. Julie Gauvin."

Watts made a mental note. A pretty young teacher arrives at work in the pre-dawn hours and is alone in an isolated portable for almost an hour on the same day a boy's body ends up nearby. It could be circumstantial, but then again…

He signaled to Bunyan to take over the questioning so he could focus on Julie's reactions. He knew that suspects often reveal far more than they realize—no matter how hard they try to hide. And this girl was hiding something. He was sure of it.

"Miss Gauvin," Bunyan said, "did you know the boy who was killed, DiAngelo D'Agosta."

Julie flinched. She couldn't help it. The sound of his name brought back ugly memories. "Yes. He was in my Period 5 literature class."

"Did you like him?" Bunyan's question caught Julie off guard.

"I can't say that I did."

The inspector jumped in. "Why is that?"

"I thought he was arrogant. He came to class late every day, and he didn't seem all that interested in his studies."

"Oh? What *was* he interested in?" From the expression on her face, Watts knew he had hit a nerve.

Julie tried to sound natural. "Goofing off, girls, typical teenage stuff."

Watts was impressed. The girl was quick on her feet. She'd said just enough without really saying anything at all.

"Thank you, Miss Gauvin." He nodded to his partner, indicating that they were ready to leave. "I'll call on you later, if I may?"

"Of course, Inspector."

As the two men turned and walked towards the door, Julie did her best to hide her relief.

A few minutes later students started filing in. It wasn't quite 7:45, but it was close enough, and Julie was too tired to object.

CHAPTER 15
POWER TRIPPERS

7:40 a.m.

Watts and Bunyan jogged up the concrete stairs to the main entrance of the school building. As pre-arranged, Velma met them there and unlocked the door.

"Hurry up! It's cold," she said, shooing them inside.

"January has a tendency to be that way," the young detective said, good-naturedly.

Velma turned her face upwards to catch a glimpse of the young man speaking to her. He was new, and a welcome relief from the other one—the frumpy middle aged one wearing heavily scuffed shoes and a wrinkled jacket that barely made it across his Buddha-like belly. How a man like that got to be Staff Inspector of Homicide, she couldn't imagine. Maybe he had contacts in upper management. It had always worked for her.

The two men hustled to keep up with Velma as she led them down the hallway, the heels of her designer Jimmy Choo's clicking on the buffed tile.

Have a seat." She nodded towards some extra chairs she had placed on the other side of her desk. "I don't believe we've been introduced." Velma offered her hand to the young detective. "I'm the Vice Principal here, Velma Vorchek. And you are?"

"Detective Paul Bunyan," he said, griping her hand firmly.

She was about to engage him in conversation, when Watts cut her off.

"Ms. Vorchek, I'm going to need those lists I asked you for yesterday."

Velma gave him a cold stare. "Give me a minute." She stalked into the outer office.

"Power tripper," Bunyan chuckled.

"Power tripper? Is that what they're calling them these days?"

A few minutes later she was back. "Here's the information you requested," she said brusquely.

Watts silently studied the information on Dino's time table. "Did you know the deceased well?" he said without looking up from his reading.

"Not particularly."

Student Body

The inspector frowned. This was the second person who had lied to him this morning, and it wasn't even eight o'clock.

"I'd like to begin the interrogations this morning," he informed her. "Paul and I will be moving into Principal Morris's office for questioning."

"This is a high school, Inspector. You can't just leave classes unattended while their teachers are being interviewed by the police."

Watts tilted his head. "Doesn't this school have 'on call' teachers who can step in whenever the regular teacher is away from the classroom?"

"You can't always count on that," she said snippily.

"I see." He thought a minute. "Well, in that case, if no 'on call' teacher is available, I'm sure that as the designated authority at Fairmont, you would be willing to assist the police by covering the classes yourself."

Velma looked aghast. "You can't be serious! Me, an *on call*!"

"I wish there was another way, but you did want to leave the school open, and I do have a job to do." He looked her squarely in the eye. "I realize our being here is a source of great inconvenience for you, Ms. Vorchek, but a boy is dead. And that's about as serious as it gets. You *do* understand that?"

Velma turned her face away. He was right, of course, but she hated it! "Okay, who do you want to see first?" she said frostily.

"I noticed that two of the grade 12 teachers share the same spare. I believe we can minimize disruption to the classes by interviewing them one at a time before the lunch period begins." He turned to Bunyan. "Let's go," he said standing up.

"Just a minute," Velma said, reaching for the phone. "I need to tell my secretary I'll be unavailable for the rest of the day. You're probably going to need my assistance."

"Thanks all the same, Ms. Vorchek, but that won't be necessary." Watts's voice was polite but firm. "Detective Bunyan and I can handle it."

"As you wish," she said, pushing back her chair and heading for the door.

The moment she was gone, Bunyan started shaking his head ruefully. "Power trippers."

"Yeah, right, power trippers," Watts mumbled under his breath.

CHAPTER 16
THE WAYWARD COASTER

10:05 a.m.

A neatly groomed, white-haired woman rapped lightly on the slightly opened door to Principal Morris's office.

"Inspector Watts?" she said before moving tentatively to an empty chair. "I'm Elaine Richardson."

Watts stood up to greet her. "That's right, and this is my partner, Detective Bunyan," he replied.

Paul politely offered his hand. "Miss Richardson."

"It's Mrs." Elaine gently corrected the young officer. "I'm a widow."

"We know you were DiAngelo D'Agosta's math teacher," the inspector began. "Can you tell us what kind of student he was? Conscientious? Hardworking? Did he make good grades?"

Elaine thought a minute. She wondered if she was being led into a trap. It *was* possible. It had happened once before, and now she was someone she didn't even recognize. Someone filled with fear.

"Well...," she said, choosing her words carefully, "the boy struggled with math to the point of needing tutoring in order to pass the course. I tried to help him by giving him lessons a few days after school—I was just doing my job," she added, as if she needed to justify herself.

Both men noticed she was becoming defensive. Watts signaled to his partner to take over. He knew the young detective had a knack for putting people at ease.

"Mrs. Richardson," Paul began, "you seemed distressed just now when you mentioned helping the boy after school. Did something go wrong during the tutoring sessions, something that may have frightened you?"

Elaine needed to get a grip. This nice young policeman was waiting for an answer, and she couldn't tell him the whole truth. But maybe, if she were careful, she could tell him part of it.

"Well, Detective, at first I thought he was just an ordinary kid, no different from all the others I tutored over the years. But I was wrong." She paused to collect her thoughts. "You see, the boy was something of a con artist. He wanted the credit for the course, but he didn't want to work for it. After a while, I felt foolish for even trying to help him. Foolish...

and used." She didn't know why she said that last bit, but it *was* the truth.

Both men immediately grasped the significance of her words and realized they would have to proceed very cautiously.

Watts was framing his next question in his mind when, without warning, Elaine jumped out of her chair and dashed over to the credenza against the wall. While the men watched in astonishment, she reached for a round wooden object lying beside some books. She pressed it to her heart and then, inexplicably, she began to weep.

"I can't believe it," she said in a voice barely above a whisper after returning to her chair. "I thought this was gone forever."

Watts and Bunyan stared intently at the object in Elaine's trembling hand. The woman's behavior was strange, to say the least, and both wondered if the object she was caressing was somehow linked to the case. They waited patiently while Elaine dabbed at her eyes with a wadded up tissue.

"I guess you're wondering what this is," she said, struggling to regain her composure.

Watts nodded to the shaken woman.

"This is my coaster," Elaine began in a faltering voice. "Actually, it's more than just a coaster. It's a memento of the early days of my marriage and of the little dog my husband and I shared back when we were newlyweds." She stopped to stare lovingly at it.

"Mrs. Richardson," Watts asked the obvious. "What's it doing in the principal's office?"

"That's exactly what I was wondering, Inspector." Actually she did have a suspicion—an ugly one—but she decided to keep that thought to herself.

Watts watched her closely. "When was the last time you saw your coaster?"

"I believe it was over the Christmas break."

"What makes you think that, Mrs. Richardson?"

"Well, we had two weeks off from work, and I used the time to do a little socializing. I had several people over to my home."

"Were any of your guests members of the staff here at Fairmont?"

"No. They were personal friends I had known for years and a few family members."

"Did you use the coaster during this two-week period of socializing?"

"I'm pretty sure I did. I usually bring them out when I entertain."

"When did you first notice the coaster was missing?"

"It was when I was doing a clean-up after the holiday. I searched and searched, hour after hour." She started twisting her hands in her lap.

Student Body

"And you haven't seen the coaster again until now?"

"That's right, Inspector," she said. Suddenly her whole body seemed to deflate as if talking about her coaster had sapped all of her strength.

Watts watched her silently for a second or two. Finally, he stood up. "I think that's all for now, Mrs. Richardson. You may go. We're going to need to keep your coaster for the time being."

"You want to test it for fingerprints?" she asked nervously.

"It's usual procedure." He paused. "Thank you for coming in. We might call on you again—is that a problem?"

"Oh no, not at all, Inspector," she said, taking tentative steps towards the door. "Not at all," she repeated as she disappeared out of the room.

"Did you believe her story?" Bunyan asked curiously.

"It's too soon to tell," Mike replied.

He moved to the door and stuck his head out.

"I wonder if you wouldn't mind stepping inside for a moment, Ms. Vorchek," he said to the VP who was chatting up the attendance secretary in the outer office.

Reluctantly she joined the two detectives in Morris's office. "We've finished our interview with Mrs. Richardson, and we'd like your professional opinion," Watts said as soon as she sat down.

Velma's eyes lit up. It was about time someone consulted her. After all, she was the one with real expertise around here. "So, what would you like to know, Inspector?"

"Does Mrs. Richardson get along with the rest of the staff? Cause trouble for the secretaries? That sort of thing…"

"As far as I know, she gets along with everybody. I've never heard any complaints."

"She's trustworthy?"

"I guess so. Why?"

"She spotted a coaster that belongs to her in this office, and she says she has no idea how it got here."

Velma's eyes grew large. "That's strange. I don't understand it myself."

"You don't?"

"Of course not! How could I?"

"Well, you have access to this office. It seems likely that you would know something about it."

"I'm not the only person who comes into this office. There's the secretaries and the caretaking staff. Any number of people could have come in here and placed that coaster there," she huffed.

"And where is *there* exactly, Ms. Vorchek?"

Velma visibly blanched.

"It's just an expression. I meant wherever you found it." She began to stand up. "Now, if you don't have any more questions for me, I'd like to get back to my own office."

Watts took notice of the woman's discomfort and decided to take his time before answering. "You may go," he said at last.

The inspector's dismissive attitude rankled her, but she held her tongue. He might bring up that damn business about the missing coaster again.

"Oh, Ms. Vorchek," he called after her as she was nearing the exit, "on your way out, please notify Ms. Malinsky we're ready for her now."

Vera spun around. "Magda wasn't one of Dino's teachers. What do you want with *her*?"

"Police business."

Her eyes blazed with fury.

Men! God, how she hated them!

CHAPTER 17
MAGDA

10:40 a.m.

"You wished to see me, Inspector?"

A somewhat formidable looking woman clutching a walking stick was standing in the doorway. She projected a unique blend of feminine and masculine energies—sort of like one of Kathy Bates' offbeat movie characters but with a greater grip on reality.

"Ms. Malinsky?" Watts stood up to acknowledge her presence. "Please have a seat. We have a few questions about the boy who was found murdered in the open field next to the school parking lot—DiAngelo D'Agosta."

"I wasn't one of his teachers. Why would you want to speak to me?" She paused. "And it's Miss."

"We already know the murder victim wasn't in any of your classes, *Miss* Malinsky. You were called down because we want to touch base with a few of the teachers at the senior

Student Body

grade level," the inspector explained. "Now, have you ever had any encounters with the D'Agosta boy?

Magda considered the matter. Either he was fishing and didn't know a thing, or he knew more than he was letting on. She turned her attention to the man she didn't recognize.

"And who are you?" she asked, not impolitely.

"I'm sorry I didn't introduce myself sooner, Miss Malinsky. "I'm Inspector Watts's partner, Detective Paul Bunyan. At your service, ma'am."

Magda's eyes danced merrily. "*You're* Paul Bunyan?"

"I know. I know." He started to laugh. "Everyone is taken aback when they hear it."

"Ahem." Mike signaled that he wanted to get down to business. "About the late Mr. D'Agosta. Did you ever have any contact with him?"

"As a matter of fact, I did."

The men waited, expecting Magda to fill them in, but she maintained an attitude of silence. It became quickly apparent that this was a woman who could not be pushed.

"Care to elaborate, Miss Malinsky?"

Magda cleared her throat and began to speak. "It was the first day of Term Two around the beginning of December, and Dino—the late Mr. D'Agosta—came to see me. He wanted to get into my biology class but it was already filled, so I told him it wasn't possible." She stopped to think about how much she wanted to reveal of that particular incident.

"Please go on, Miss Malinsky," the young detective encouraged her.

"Well, not to put too fine a point on it," she said, "the boy tried to seduce me into getting the answer he wanted. To tell you the truth, I was rather shocked by his behaviour, but I had the impression that he had done this sort of thing before and had been successful at it."

"But he wasn't successful with you, is that right?" Watts said.

"Do you see his name on my list of students for this term?"

Watts resisted the urge to smile. *Tough. Definitely tough.*

"Miss Malinsky," he said, "would you tell us what you thought of Dino? Was there anything about him that might make someone want to kill him?"

"Frankly, I can't think of anyone on staff who *didn't* want to kill him."

"We're rapidly coming to that conclusion ourselves," Watts said dryly. "Could you give us an example of Dino's unsavory behavior?"

"All right, I'll be blunt. This seventeen-year-old kid told me to my face that if I gave in to his request to join my science class, he would take me to a motel and fuck my brains out—to be more or less precise. And that's when I gave him a little biology lesson of my own."

Watts didn't blink. "What did you do?"

"I showed him a move in martial arts that would kill him in seconds. That shut him up, I can tell you."

"Miss Malinsky," Mike said solemnly, "did you kill him?"

"No."

"But you *did* threaten him?"

"Yes... and no. Like all cocky people, he was a coward. It wasn't necessary to kill him. All I had to do was scare him."

"I know you implied everyone on staff pretty much hated this kid, but I'm curious..." Paul leaned in closer. "Who do you *think* killed him, Miss Malinsky?"

Magda grew quiet. That was a question she had been wondering about herself.

"I don't know," she said slowly. "But I rather suspect it was someone really close to him. Of course, that could have been any number of people on staff."

"I see." The inspector studied her thoughtfully. "Do you drive to school," he said, shifting the topic of conversation, "or do you take public transit?"

"Neither," she said. "If you must know, I walk. It's good for my legs."

"You walk every day, including yesterday?"

"Unfortunately not," she said ruefully. "The snowstorm made that too dangerous for me to navigate the city streets. My mother drove me."

"She let you off at the front of the school?"

"She wanted to, but that wasn't possible. Snowplows were blocking the road, so I directed her to the teachers' parking lot at the back of the school. And if your next question is 'what time was that', I'm guessing somewhere around 6 to 6:15."

Watts arched his eyebrows. "Why so early, Miss Malinsky?"

"Mom wanted to get back home before rush-hour hit, and I needed to do some last-minute prep."

"Did you see anyone in the parking lot when you arrived?"

"Not really. Sorry, Inspector," she said honestly. "I wish I could be more helpful."

"One last question, Miss Malinsky. What was your most powerful impression of the deceased? Was there anything about him specifically that might have given someone a motive for murder?"

Magda sighed. She had already painted a pretty bleak image of the boy. Why not complete the picture?

"Dino had no scruples. He exploited people and then discarded them when he got what he wanted. In my opinion, the boy was a bottom feeder, and I can't help but believe the world is better off without him."

Student Body

If the detectives were shocked by her answer, they didn't show it. It was obvious the woman had strong feelings where the victim was concerned. But could she have acted on them? That was the question.

"I think we're done here," Watts said, watching her closely as she rose from her chair, leaning on her walking stick for support.

"Your walking stick is very unusual," he said. "I've never seen that shade of wood before. What is it? Cherry?"

"No, it's rosewood," she said proudly. "I used to rely on a cane to get around, but then I developed arthritis in my wrists and the handle became too awkward to use. My parents were aware of this problem, so when they went to Rio de Janeiro for their fiftieth wedding anniversary last summer, they saw this walking stick, and bought it for me."

"You found that an improvement?"

"Very much so. As you can see, the top of the walking stick has a thick head but right below it the wood is tapered to fit the grip of a human hand. Unlike a cane, I can grasp the walking stick below the wide head without having to bend my wrist. The fact that it is a beautiful piece of wood is just a bonus," she said looking at it fondly.

" It *is* striking," Watts agreed. He stood up and offered her his hand.

Magda was a bit taken aback. Why would the inspector want to shake hands with her? It did seem odd. Still, she decided to oblige him.

Suddenly it felt like her fingers were being crushed in a metal compactor. But she didn't pull away. Instead, she applied equal force to the man squeezing her hand until it was he who disengaged first.

Once outside the office, Magda's mind was spinning. It had been the inspector's idea to shake hands, and then he exerted so much pressure she had to stifle the urge to cry out. At first it didn't make any sense.

And then it hit her. He wanted to see how strong she was! Maybe her story about threatening Dino with a lethal martial arts technique had him wondering.

With a sense of disquiet, she hurried out of the main office and headed for the stairway. Using her walking stick for leverage, she hustled down the hallway and hastily climbed the stairs. Alone in her classroom, she had time to think. Had she said too much? Been too candid?

Well, what's done is done, Magda thought, turning her attention to practical matters. Her work day was about to begin.

Time to get busy.

"Do you think she could have done it?" Bunyan wondered.

"Could she have done it? No question about it," Mike said massaging his sore hand. "Did she do it? Evidence will tell. Right now we need to conduct several searches."

Paul furrowed his brow. "What was all that talk about her walking stick?"

"Just following a hunch, my boy. One of the best weapons in a cop's arsenal is his instinct."

"I see," Paul paused for a second. "Want me to see the judge about a search warrant?"

"I want you to see the judge about several warrants. Here's the list," he handed his young assistant a hand-written note. "I've already made the necessary calls, so you shouldn't have any trouble. By the way, any word on the kid's relatives?"

"None so far." The young detective started heading for the door.

"Snoop around the apartment building where the D'Agostas live. See what you can find out. Then meet me at headquarters around one o'clock," Watts called after him. "I'm going to grab a quick lunch, probably at a drive-through. You should eat something yourself. We've got a lot of work to do this afternoon."

"Right."

Mike paused. "I think I'll just have a few words with the Lady VP before I go."

"Oh?" Paul grinned. "Sorry I have to miss that."

Bev Bachmann

—

Alone in Principal Morris's office, Mike allowed his mind to sort through the known facts of the case. It was obvious to him that there were no end of suspects, all of whom were tossing the truth around like a freaking Frisbee.

What he needed was evidence—good, solid evidence based on the truth. The problem was that truth here at Fairmont High was as slippery as Toronto's icy roads. One wrong move could land you face-down in a ditch.

Or face-up in the morgue.

CHAPTER 18
"A FORCE OF NATURE"

11:25 a.m.

"I see you're alone," Velma said as she strolled into the principal's office. "So who's next on your hit parade: the lunch lady? the guy who sweeps the halls?"

Mike Watts leaned back in his chair and formed a steeple with the tips of his fingers. "As a matter of fact, *you* are," he said, pushing a chair towards her with his foot. "Have a seat."

Velma stared suspiciously at the proffered chair. "I see you spoke with our English, math, and science teachers," she said, sitting down slowly. "Did you learn anything?"

"Well, actually I learned a lot. For instance, the math teacher Mrs. Richardson was shocked to discover her coaster here in the principal's office. How do you suppose it got there?"

Velma stiffened. "Memories play tricks on us as we age, Inspector. Who knows where the woman lost it. In any case, someone here at school found the thing on the grounds and passed it on to me. I was too busy at the time to try to locate its owner, so I stashed it in Morris' office and forgot about it." She stopped to take a breath. "Anyway, why is a damned coaster so important?"

Mike ignored her question. "You never mentioned that it was you who put the coaster in the principal's office."

"I forgot." She looked daggers at him. "Anyway, what difference does it make who put what where? This is a big school. Things get misplaced all the time?"

"Everything that could be connected to a murder case is important, Ms. Vorchek." He eyed her suspiciously. "The fact of the matter is that a coaster went from being in the private home of a staff member to being placed in the principal's office, and until now, no one has taken responsibility for that happening. And you have no idea who gave you the coaster before you decided to place it on Principal Morris' credenza. Is that correct?"

Velma was starting to worry. If she were to name someone—anyone—as the person who gave the coaster to her to deal with, the Inspector would follow up and find out that she was lying. No. She had to stick with her story of not being able to remember. It was a lame explanation, but still plausible.

He studied her keenly. It was time to change tactics. "Moving on, did you know that Dino tried to seduce Miss Malinsky into allowing him into her biology class?"

Student Body

The sudden change of subject caught Velma off guard. She resorted to her favorite fallback position—her role as vice-principal. "I didn't know that, Inspector," she said, sitting up straighter. "Miss Malinsky should have come to me with this. I would have spoken to the boy."

"And what would you have said to him, exactly?" he asked coolly.

"I would have told him that his behavior was inappropriate... Obviously."

"Miss Malinsky was under the impression that Dino had tried the same seduction routine with other teachers. Were you aware of any such attempts?"

Velma fought a growing sense of alarm. "No. I wasn't aware of any such attempts."

Watts thought he detected a few beads of sweat on Velma's upper lip. He decided to push harder. "Dino was a very attractive kid. Was he not?"

"Yes. There are lots of attractive kids at Fairmont," she hastened to add.

"And how many of these 'attractive kids' come on to teachers?"

Velma turned her face away. "I don't know," she said quietly.

"I think you do know. In fact, I think you were one of them."

"That's ridiculous!" she protested hotly." If that were true, I could lose my job."

"Ms. Vorchek, what we're dealing with here is a homicide. If you're lying to me, you could lose a lot more than your job." He paused to let the words sink it.

Velma's eyes darted around the room as if searching for a means of escape. "All right. All right," she blurted out finally. "I'll tell you the truth, but it has to stay in this room, or I'm saying nothing."

"I can't promise you that, Ms. Vorchek. This is a murder investigation. But I will say this—telling me the truth is your wisest course of action at this point in time."

Velma sighed heavily. She had run out of options, and she knew it. Finally she began to speak slowly, struggling with every sentence. "Okay, Inspector. I did get the coaster from Dino. He got it when he went to Elaine's house—ostensibly for some tutoring—and when she wasn't looking, he sneaked it into his backpack. Then he brought the thing to me. He told me he wanted a high mark on the mid-term exam, and he thought he could coerce his teacher into giving it to him."

"Why did he give it to *you*? Were you in on his plan to blackmail Mrs. Richardson?"

"*No*. It was all his idea. I didn't know about it until he gave me the coaster to keep for him, and I hid it in Morris's office. I know it was stupid, but I did it because I wanted to please him. He had this *power* over me… he…" Her voice trailed off.

"You were having an affair?"

"No. That's too ugly a word. We were having a romance—a 'fine romance'—as the song says," she smiled weakly.

"And you weren't worried about losing your position with the Board?"

"You have to understand," she said quietly. "Dino was like a drug. Once he got into your system, you'd do anything for him. I can't explain it any better than that."

"I see." Mike got up from his chair and prepared to leave.

"Please, Inspector, you have to keep this a secret. If it got out I could lose everything. Please, I'm begging you. Don't say anything." The desperation in her voice was sincere, and in spite of his intense dislike of the woman, he did feel some sympathy for her. She had been played—and by one of the best.

"Ms. Vorchek," he said, "as long as your secret affair doesn't interfere with the course of justice, it can remain precisely that—a secret."

She was shaking as she stood up. "I know I sound like some kind of slut, but you had to have known Dino. He was a force of nature. No one could resist him."

"Oh?" The inspector looked her squarely in the eye. "Well, somebody did, and rather emphatically, at that."

CHAPTER 19
AT POLICE HEADQUARTERS

1:05 p.m.

"What did you find out at the D'Agosta apartment?" Mike asked while prying the lid off his Tim Horton's coffee cup.

Paul opened his spiral notebook and started scanning the pages. "Well, for starters, the only known occupant is listed as a tenant named Mary D'Agosta who has, or rather had, a son enrolled at Fairmont High School. Apparently she's been out of town for the last three days. The bartender at her workplace, a seedy dive on Lakeshore Boulevard called The Sure Thing, believes she left with a customer and the two of them drove to Chicago—at least that was what he overheard them talking about right before they left together." He flipped to the next page. "The manager hasn't been able to get in touch with her since."

"Anyone know the name of the guy she left with?" Watts said, digging around in a white paper bag for a plump strawberry-filled donut. He bit into it gingerly.

"No. The guy isn't a regular according to one of the cocktail waitresses I spoke with," Paul said, once again consulting his notes.

Watts snatched a handful of Kleenex and began blotting his mouth. "So it's possible the mother has no idea her son is dead?"

"That's a safe assumption," Paul agreed.

Mike crushed the tissues into a tight little ball and tossed it into the waste basket. "Did you get any information from any of other tenants?"

"Just innuendos and gossip. The consensus is that the mother is presumed divorced and—if you believe the neighbors—something of a 'tramp' who has a constant stream of men coming and going through her apartment. As far as I could make out, no father is listed on any official documents. It appears the mother raised Dino by herself with the aid of social assistance and the public school system. The boy was left pretty much on his own." He looked up from his notes. "That's all I got. There really isn't much to go on, Boss."

Mike thought for a moment. "Was the boy living at his mother's apartment at the time of his death?"

"No—not according to the neighbors. It seems he moved out some time before Christmas. That fact, coupled with the mother's recent disappearance, would further indicate she has no idea her son is dead."

"Okay. I want to know as soon as the mother's back in town. After that, you and I are going to pay her a little visit."

"Right."

Mike started for the door. "I need to wash up before we head to the pathologist's lab." A few minutes later he emerged from the men's room. "By the way, did you read the coroner's report?"

"Yes."

"Well, what do you think?"

"I think we need more evidence."

"That's right, my boy. A smart cop needs to do two things: one, keep an open mind, and two, follow the trail of evidence."

"Makes sense."

"Easy to forget though," said Mike as he hurried down the hall. With his long legs, Paul had no trouble keeping up.

—

When he reached the lab, Watts got right to the point. "We're here about the D'Agosta case. Can you verify the time of death?"

The busy pathologist looked up from his work. "According to my calculations the victim was killed sometime between 7:20 and 8:20 am."

Student Body

Mike nodded. This information jibed with what was written in the coroner's report. "What can you tell us about the wounds on the body?"

"Well," drawled Dr. Hardy, a slight, bespectacled man wearing a lab coat and a serious expression. "Look at this, gentlemen." He held up a plaster mold of the victim's head.

"There are indentations from two separate blows, a small wound to the temple and a larger wound to the back of the skull. The smaller wound burst some capillaries which caused a certain amount of bleeding but not enough to lead to death. The larger wound on the back of the skull was the fatal blow."

"Did you find any other injuries on the body—defensive type wounds?" Watts asked.

"No," the medical man replied. "Whoever struck this kid on the back of the head apparently did so without the boy's knowledge." Dr. Hardy took off his wire framed glasses and wiped them with a soft cloth. "The deceased was six foot two, a healthy seventeen-year-old. For someone to sneak up behind him and surprise him like that, the boy had to be either distracted or disabled."

The two detectives took a moment to process this latest information.

"What's your best guess, Doc?" Watts asked.

"My best guess is that the boy was somehow disabled," the pathologist said solemnly. "As I indicated, this is an individual who would not be that easy to kill. With his size and strength, he would have fought back fiercely. No, to take this boy by surprise, he had to have been disabled."

"Let me ask you another question. Could the assailant have been either a man or a woman?"

"Definitely."

"How can you be so sure?"

"Let me tell you about a case I was involved in a few months ago," the pathologist began patiently. "A woman who weighed approximately 98 pounds smashed her 215-pound brute of a husband over the head with a cast iron skillet, killing him instantly. It happened like this. Just before she called him down to breakfast, she slipped some of her crushed sleeping tablets into a bowl of eggs she was whisking with a fork. She knew he was in the habit of pouring hot sauce over everything and that it would cover up any sense of an unusual taste. Then, as soon as the husband sat down and started eating, he suddenly slumped face down into his plate of scrambled eggs. That was when she conked him over the head. It was lights out time."

"She got away with it?" Paul asked incredulously.

"Not exactly. The jury felt pity for her because of the years of abuse she had endured, so they gave her a light sentence. Some said it was a miscarriage of justice, others felt he got what was coming to him. Who knows? I deal in facts. I don't judge."

Student Body

Mike considered the doc's words carefully. "Are there any other facts that lead you to believe the D'Agosta boy was disabled and couldn't defend himself?"

"First, there is the fact that the wound on the back of the skull was placed high up on the head. To do that, an assailant would have to have been taller than, or at least as tall as, the deceased. If that were the case, the boy would certainly have sensed someone coming up behind him and spun around in time to fight back. The fact that he didn't leads me to believe that he was much lower in elevation than his assailant—an unlikely prospect, given the victim's height. However, a different scenario suggests itself."

"Which is?"

"I think the boy was either slouched over or on his knees when the attack came."

"On his knees?"

"More than likely," the doctor reaffirmed.

"So, perhaps there were two assailants—one to distract, or disable if you will—and one to attack? Is that your conclusion?"

"It's hard to say at this point. At the moment, all we have is conjecture."

Mike furrowed his brow. "So, based on what we know so far, there might have been one, or there might have been two assailants. And either assailant could have been male or female. Is that what you're saying?"

"Yes. It would appear so."

"Well, that certainly narrows it down," Watts said dryly. He decided to explore another aspect of the case. "Let's talk about the murder weapon. Got any thoughts?"

"Yes, I do," Dr. Hardy confirmed. "It was something in the shape of a rolling pin."

"A rolling pin?" Both detectives looked surprised.

"Actually a wooden mallet is the more probable murder weapon," Dr. Hardy explained. "I mentioned a rolling pin because the type of mallet you would find in a wood carving kit looks like half a rolling pin. In any case, the weapon was definitely made out of wood."

The detectives were intrigued. "What makes you so sure?"

"Inside the wound on the back of the victim's scalp we found microscopic traces of wood."

"Can you identify the type of wood?"

"It's rosewood."

"Rosewood? Is that kind of wood typically used to make carving mallets?"

"Yes," the pathologist confirmed. "It's standard."

"There's one more thing," Dr. Hardy added. "Rosewood is not indigenous to North America."

"Oh," the inspector's eyes widened. "Where is it indigenous to?"

"Countries where the climate tends to be tropical—India, Jamaica, Honduras, Brazil…"

Watts turned to Bunyan and nodded. It was time to leave. "Thanks, you've been a big help," he said, heading for the exit with Bunyan right behind him.

CHAPTER 20
FIATS AND FERRARIS

2:45 p.m.

Back at Fairmont, Watts and Bunyan once again settled in the principal's office. It was almost the end of the school day, and Armand Saint-Yves was standing stiffly in the doorway. He had been summoned for questioning, and he wasn't the least bit happy about it.

"I really don't know why I'm here," he said, looking around sullenly.

"You're here because I sent for you," Watts replied coolly. "Have a seat."

Armand took a few reluctant steps into the room. "I had to leave my class unattended because no 'on call' was available," he said, cautiously lowering himself into a grey metal chair. "You do realize school ends in half hour, and students could take advantage of my absence to cut out early."

"We'll have to chance it," Watts said drolly.

Armand shrugged. "So what do you want from me? I already gave my statement to the police yesterday. I have nothing more to add." He crossed his arms in front of his chest as if the matter had been sufficiently settled.

The inspector studied the small, wiry man sitting on the other side of the principal's desk. "Well," he said casually, "it's always possible to forget a few details. I thought you and I might have a little chat to clear a few things up."

Armand crossed one leg languidly over the over. "Go ahead, Inspector. I've got nothing to hide."

"On the day of the murder, at what time did you arrive at school?"

"I'm not sure exactly. Somewhere around 7:30 am."

"Did anyone see you pull in?"

"I doubt it. It was snowing pretty hard."

"So, according to your best recollection, you arrived at the parking lot at 7:30 am. Is that the time you usually arrive?"

"Oh heavens, no! I overslept that morning and was running quite late."

"What did you do after you parked your car?"

"Well, I was a bit flustered because I had to run off some photocopies in the main office, and there wasn't much time before classes started."

"Are you saying you immediately went to the main building when you got out of your car?"

"No. I went to my portable first and unlocked it. Then I jotted down a note on the board to the effect that I would be right back." He paused. "Sometimes if the students don't see you in the classroom through the window, they bugger off for a smoke and then lose track of time."

Armand twisted around so that he was facing the door. "Is this going to take much longer? If I don't get back soon, there may not be a class left."

"So you mentioned." The inspector dismissed Armand's concerns and leaned back in his chair as if he had all the time in the world. "So, let me get this straight. You got out of your car, went to your classroom, unlocked the door, and then left a brief note on the blackboard. Is that correct?"

"Yes. That's right."

"I see." Watts looked thoughtful. "On your way to the office in the main building, did you notice anything unusual?"

"Not really. You have to remember that visibility was practically non-existent. It was a bitch of a storm, I can tell you."

So far the man's story made sense. However, Watts couldn't help feeling that something was *off*. "On your way to and from your portable, did you see anyone staggering around in the parking lot?"

"Staggering?! Of course not!" Armand seemed incensed. "Teachers don't usually come to work drunk, Inspector." He stopped to brush a tiny speck of lint off the pocket of his Brooks Brothers shirt.

"At what time did you leave the main building and return to your classroom?"

"I don't know. Maybe 8:00 am. I can't be sure."

"Between the time you say you arrived at school, around 7:30 am, and the time you think you left the main building at 8:00 am, you saw no one in the vacant field beside the parking lot?"

"I couldn't say. I was focused on my footing in the heavy snowfall. And nothing else," he added emphatically. "That's the god's honest truth, Inspector."

The inspector stared at his suspect. The man could be telling the truth. Sometimes things that sound improbable actually do turn out to be *the god's honest truth*. "Okay," he said, "let's leave the scene of the parking lot for a moment. We know you were one of the deceased's teachers. What can you tell us about him?"

"Dino?" Armand started stroking his goatee until the point was as sharp as a watercolor paint brush. "What do you want to know about him?"

"How did he strike you?"

"What do you mean?"

"What I mean is did you like him?"

The question intrigued Armand. He began rubbing his forehead thoughtfully. "You wouldn't understand, Inspector. Dino wasn't someone to be liked or disliked."

Armand paused. It was such a struggle to find the right words that would explain the ill-fated boy.

"Dino wasn't like other people, Inspector. He was different. He was… unique… exquisite—something to be savored like a fine wine or a priceless work of art."

"Are you saying you *liked* him?" Watts asked in a strained voice.

Armand studied his fingernails with absorbed fascination. "Let me put it this way, Inspector, DiAngelo D'Agosta was a Ferrari in a world full of Fiats."

The inspector said nothing. Whatever his thoughts were, he was keeping to himself. A few seconds went by in silence.

"I see," he said finally. "Two more questions, Mr. Saint-Yves, and then you can go."

"Yes?"

"Have you ever been in the school's shop?"

"Once, unfortunately. It was late November, near the end of the term, and Gunther had to go to court for his divorce."

Watts was curious. "Why 'unfortunately'?"

"Well, first of all, the shop is the filthiest place in the school. And, second of all, it's dangerous! That place is a chamber of horrors—full of nasty table saws and razor sharp tools." Armand shuddered. "Hollywood would have a field day with—"

"I get the picture," Watts said, cutting him off. "Now Mr. Saint-Yves, to my next question. "Do you own a wood-carving set?"

"Are you kidding?!" Armand's shoulders shook with indignation. "What do you think I am? Some kind of stone-age relic like Grossman? Get real!"

Watts had heard enough. He pushed his chair back abruptly to indicate the meeting was over. "Thanks for coming, Mr. Saint-Yves. You may go."

Armand stood up stiffly and took a few faltering steps towards the door. Just then the final school bell pierced the ensuing silence with the jolt of a dentist's drill. It was music to his ears.

—

"So," Mike said, swiveling around to face his assistant who had been standing in a corner of the room quietly observing the interview. "What do you think?"

"I'm not sure." Paul shook his head thoughtfully. "Bit of a drama queen, but is he our killer? I just don't know."

"Did you believe his answers?"

"That's the problem," Bunyan said. "With people like that—types who thrive on attention—you just never know. Drama queens, like Mr. Saint-Yves, often omit details they deem dull or boring. Their priority is applause, not accuracy. So, to answer your question: did I believe his story? Yes and no."

"You're a big help."

The young detective shrugged. "So, what did *you* think of our Mr. Armand Saint-Yves?"

"What did I think?" Mike snorted. "I think the man's a Fiat who fancies himself a Ferrari."

Paul laughed out loud. "Yes, but is he capable of murder?"

"As you said earlier, we need evidence before coming to any conclusions." Watts got up to stretch his back. It had been a long day, and it wasn't over yet. He picked up the office phone. "I think it's time to have a little talk with our last suspect."

Paul looked amused. " You don't mean …?"

"Who else?" Mike said, cupping his hand over the receiver. "The stone-age relic."

CHAPTER 21
TOOLS OF THE TRADE

3:35 p.m.

Gunther pulled up a chair and plopped down into it like a sack of cement. "Listen, Inspector, I'm exhausted, and I got a dozen football players waiting for me in the gym. Do you think we can make this quick?"

"Sure," the inspector said agreeably. "Shall we get started?" He waited until he had Gunther's full attention. "We know the deceased, DiAngelo D'Agosta, was one of your students. What can you tell us about him?"

"Dino?" Gunther leaned back in his chair and stared up at the ceiling as if he were watching the boy on a moving picture screen. "You want to talk about Dino? Well, for starters, he was in my shop class for a while. Showed up whenever he damn well pleased, so I dropped him from the course. Cockiest kid I ever met! A real smart ass!"

"Then it's safe to say you didn't like him?"

"Like him? It wasn't a question of liking him—at least, not at first. The truth is I was amused by his rather cocky mannerisms, and then one day after school he told me about his home life. It sounded miserable to me—a lot like my own childhood—so, I guess I felt sorry for him. But then, after I did what I could to make his life a little easier, he turned on me. He actually seemed to take pleasure in making me look like a fool. I soon realized that I had been had. And, after that, I came to loathe him," Gunther spit the words out like a bad taste in his mouth.

The force of Gunther's response caused Watts to pause. "Let's go back to the day of the murder," he said. "What time did you arrive at school?"

"I pulled into the parking lot at 6:30 am. I do that once in a while when the class is starting a new project," he explained. "I had to pull out the equipment they were going to use that day and pre-cut some wood." Gunther reached down to adjust his pant leg which had bunched up at the crotch.

Watts pretended not to notice. "Were you alone when you arrived at your portable?"

"Yes. As a rule, kids don't like getting up that early, Inspector. Anyway, I unlocked the door and got out the wood I needed for the new assignment and started working."

"Did you stay in your portable from the time you say arrived at 6:30 am until 8:15 when students have to be in class?"

"No. After I pre-cut the wood and organized the kits, I locked the door and left."

"And what time was that?"

"Well, I wasn't looking at my watch, but I would guess around 7:00 am or so."

"Did anyone see you while you were in your portable between 6:30 and 7:00 am?"

"I don't think so, but I can't be sure."

"Now, Mr. Grossman, after you left your portable at, or near, 7 am, where did you go?"

"I needed a jolt of joe, so I hightailed it to the nearest Tim's on Queen Street."

"Is this a regular haunt of yours?"

"Yeah. Why?"

"We're going to need the location of the coffee shop where you went the morning of the murder." Watts nodded to his partner who got out his pen in anticipation of Gunther's answer.

"Okay," Gunther said, dictating the requested information as Bunyan wrote in his trusty notebook. "Are we almost finished, Inspector? I hate to keep the guys waiting. Some of them need to get to part-time jobs." He began tugging at his pant leg which had twisted itself around his thigh.

"Just a few more questions, Mr. Grossman," he said, "and then you're free to go. Do you always lock your classroom when you're not there?"

"Yes. There are a lot of expensive tools in the shop. Can't have anybody just wandering in."

"So you yourself need to be present when students are in the classroom?"

"That's right."

"Can students take their projects home and work on them there?"

"Sure, if their parents can afford the appropriate tools," he said. "But not everybody has that kind of money."

The inspector eyed him curiously. "If the tools are so valuable, how do you prevent pilfering when your back is turned?"

"The tools are kept on the wall when not in use. Each tool has an outline of its shape so the kids know where to return them. Just before the end of class, they hang up the tools on the corresponding outlines. If any tool is missing, I know immediately a kid has tried to snatch it."

The inspector was intrigued. "And how do you know that any tool you find in a student's possession is one that belongs to the school?"

Gunther settled back, visibly relaxed. "That's easy. I use something called a Dremel 1550 Versa Tip to identify the tools. You see, Inspector, the Dremel is an engraver which holds a hot knife. We use it to carve designs in wood and other materials."

Student Body

He seemed suddenly charged with energy. "Let me tell you about the Dremel—a great little tool. You can use it to carve the numbers of your address on a plank of wood and then hang it in your front yard or you can carve an owl or a racoon or a—"

"What does any of this have to do with my question?" Watts asked.

"Sorry. I get carried away sometimes," he said with a sheepish grin. "The Dremel is just so versatile and—"

"You still haven't answered my question," the inspector said somewhat irritably. "What does the Dremel have to do with keeping tabs on mallets that belong to the school?"

"Simple," Gunther smiled confidently. "I use it to carve the school's initials in tiny letters on each tool. All I have to do is look for the tiny letters FH on the bottom of the handle of a wooden mallet, and I know all I need to know. Piece of cake," he said, a smile of satisfaction on his face.

Watts looked thoughtful. "Okay. Now let's talk about the rest of the staff. You say that on the morning of the murder, you arrived at your portable, unlocked the door, and remained there for approximately thirty minutes. If a member of the staff had pulled into the parking lot about that time, would they have noticed that your portable was open?"

"As I already mentioned, the light was on, so it's possible."

"After you left Tim Horton's, where did you go?"

"Back to school." He shifted uncomfortably in his seat. "I really do need to get to the gym, Inspector."

Watts took note of the fact that his suspect was getting restless. It was a good sign. When a man got tired, he was more likely to make mistakes.

The questions continued. "When you got back to the school after your trip to Tim's, did you go to the main office or to your portable?"

"The office." He paused. "Inspector, the guys are waiting for me!" For the first time Gunther felt uncertain. It was beginning to dawn on him that he didn't have an alibi for the times between his arrival at school at 6:30 and the beginning of period one at 8:15. He looked around nervously.

Mike kept up the pressure. "Did anyone see you when you were in the main building—someone who might be willing to vouch for the time you were there?"

"I wasn't paying attention to anyone I might have seen in the hallways, Inspector. It was getting late and I was in a hurry." Gunther could feel his sweatshirt sticking to his back like a damp towel. "All I can say is I had to be in the building to collect my mail—as all teachers have to—before 8:15 am because that's when period one begins."

Several seconds slid by in silence as the inspector watched him with studied indifference. Gunther found the quiet unnerving. He was actually hoping for more questions—anything to break the tension of waiting.

Student Body

That wasn't what happened.

Without warning, the inspector pushed back his chair and stood up.

"That's all for now Mr. Grossman. You may go," the inspector said, summarily dismissing the shop teacher.

Up to this point Gunther had been waiting for the chance to bolt from the room, but suddenly he felt reluctant to leave—as if nothing had been settled, at least nothing in his favor.

He got up slowly and started for the exit. As he did, he passed the inspector's tall, taciturn assistant leaning beside the door, his arms folded casually across his chest.

"Paul Bunyan, huh? It fits."

—

"Excuse me, Inspector," Velma Vorchek's secretary stuck her head in the door. "There's a call for you. Shall I transfer it in here?"

Watts nodded politely, then picked up the receiver. "Yes... Okay... Get in touch with the super and tell him we're on our way... Thanks." He hung up the phone and turned to his young assistant. "Do you have those search warrants I ordered?"

"Right here." Paul patted his coat pocket. "What's up?"

"That was a message from headquarters. Seems Mary D'Agosta's *date* is finally over."

CHAPTER 22
MARY D'AGOSTA

5:25 p.m.

"What the hell are you doing in here?" A tall woman with hair the color of blood oranges filled the narrow doorway, a soiled navy suitcase sitting at her feet. She was staring sullenly at two men coming out of her son's bedroom.

"The super let us in," Watts said simply. "Mrs. D'Agosta?"

"That's right," she snarled. "Who the fuck are you?!"

"I'm Staff Inspector Watts of Toronto's Homicide Squad and this is Detective Bunyan." He turned to his assistant. "Show Mrs. D'Agosta the search warrant." The woman stretched out a scrawny hand covered with purple veins thick as worms and snatched at the paper.

"Perhaps you should sit down, Mrs. D'Agosta," Paul said gently. "We have some bad news." His eyes scanned the apartment looking for a seat that wasn't buried under a pile of rumpled clothes or greasy pizza boxes. "Here's a spot," he said, brushing debris off a worn living room chair with a broad sweep of his arm.

Mary D'Agosta didn't budge. "If you're looking for drugs, I got nothing to hide," she sneered, giving both men a look of loathing. "I been clean for six months."

"We're not here to look for drugs," Paul said quietly. "It's about your son." He waited until he was sure he had her complete attention before continuing. "The boy was murdered outside his school, and we're investigating the crime." It was a lot to take in, and he paused to let her absorb the shock.

This wasn't the first time the young detective had been recruited to deliver this kind of news, and each time he had no idea of what to expect. Reactions varied vastly. Some just collapsed into a heap of despair. Others simply shut down. But no one had ever reacted as if what they were hearing was nothing more noteworthy than the weather report. Until today.

The woman said nothing for a minute, then she pulled out a flask of vodka from her handbag and took a swig. "Murdered, huh?" She took another swig. "So which one of his bitches did him in?"

The young detective was momentarily taken aback. "I beg your pardon?"

"Come on, if you two are 'on the case,' you have to know by now that Dino was—what's the male term for slut—I mean the guy would screw anything with a pulse. You know

Student Body

what I mean?" She looked from one cop to the other. They didn't respond. "Sure, he was a good looking kid, but keep his pecker in his pants—in a school full of horny teenagers, not to mention some of the swinging teachers who were after him—not a chance!" She upended the flask for the third time.

Watts didn't blink. "Did Dino have a steady girlfriend or a best friend he confided in?"

"The answer is 'no.' Say, what are you two doing here anyway? You said Dino was killed at school. What does that have to do with *me*—or this apartment—which I locked him out of, by the way, right before school closed for the holidays. Didn't want him hanging 'round during daylight hours while I'm... busy. Besides, he was a messy kid," she chuckled.

Watts's expression was deadpan. "We searched his room," he said, taking a step towards her, "and we found something." He showed her a small white box.

"What's that?" She belched loudly, alcohol fumes fanning the air. Instinctively Watts backed away.

"A jewelry box containing four solid gold chains. I'm not an expert," Watts said, "but I would estimate the total value of these chains to be close to three thousand dollars."

"What! You mean to tell me that little prick was holding out on me?!"

The inspector ignored her outburst. "By the way, did you buy the chains for him?"

"Are you insane?! Do you think I'd live in a dump like this if I could afford to buy gold jewelry?"

"Then where did he get the money?"

"You have to ask? What kind of cops are you anyway? Obviously the boy was turning tricks—or had some sugar daddy shooting his wad in thousand dollar bills." She took another slug of Vodka. "Beats working for a livin."

"Did he ever mention any names?" Watts asked, disregarding her crude remarks.

"No, he didn't. Wouldn't have been smart, now would it?" She shook her head in disgust. God, these cops were clueless.

Watts signaled it was time to go, but there was one more bit of business to take care of.

"About Dino's body," he said bluntly, "it's in the city morgue. You can claim it at any time for burial."

She exploded with an unexpected rage. "You shitting me?!" she shrieked. "I can't afford no funeral!"

"You could get a loan," Paul suggested, trying to be helpful. "Use the gold chains as collateral."

Mary D'Agosta gave that idea some thought. "Nope! Belonged to my son. Gonna keep it to remember him by."

"That's very big of you, Mrs. D'Agosta," Watts said dryly. "So are you going to claim the body, or are you going to let the government bury your boy?"

"The gov'ment can have him," she said flatly. "Boy's no good to me dead." She turned her back on them and began walking unsteadily towards her bedroom. "I been on the road eight hours straight, and I need to get some sleep."

"Right." The men were poised at the threshold when Watts turned around. "Anything you'd like to add before we leave, Mrs. D'Agosta?"

"Yeah! Don't come back here. Cops seen hanging 'round the building—it ain't good for business."

Bunyan looked puzzled. "I thought you said you were a cocktail waitress."

"Yeah. That's right. A cocktail waitress."

She burst into hysterical laughter as if she had just said the wittiest thing in the world and then disappeared on the other side of her bedroom door where she continued to cackle maniacally.

—

The two officers stood in the apartment hallway getting their bearings.

"So that was Mary D'Agosta," Mike said, shaking his head as if to dislodge the image of the woman from his brain.

"Not exactly a candidate for mother of the year, is she?"

Watts cracked a smile. "Well, in spite of her lack of cooperation, we did discover something that could provide an important clue."

"The jewelry?"

"That's right. It's odd he didn't take the chains with him when he left his mother's apartment," Watts said. "But then she *did* say she locked him out. I suspect his chains were still inside."

"He probably intended to return and wheedle his way back into the apartment to get them," Bunyan said.

"I agree. In any case, we need to find the jewelers who sold the chains and get copies of the bill of sale."

"I'm on my way," Paul said, taking big strides towards the elevator.

CHAPTER 23
"THE LED DOESN'T LIE"

9:27 p.m.

Watts and Bunyan stood back, watching Harold McCormick, the head of the forensic unit, finish his work.

"Thanks for coming on such short notice, Hal."

A serious looking grey haired man was packing up his forensic kit inside the school's shop portable. "You're welcome, Mike. I owed you a favor," he said good-naturedly. "But why now, and why at night?"

"I needed privacy."

"Ah, a covert operation." He grinned and pulled off his rubber gloves, shoving them inside his lab coat pocket.

"So, what'd you find?"

"The light-emitting diode showed no traces of blood anywhere on the wood carving kit," Hal answered. "These mallets contain nothing but wood—no biological tissue of any kind."

Mike looked puzzled. "Are you sure?"

"Listen, the LED doesn't lie. If there's blood on any of these mallets—no matter how long ago it first appeared—it will show up as a blue luminescence light on the surface. I thoroughly checked all the mallets in the wood carving set as you requested, and no traces of blood showed up. You won't find the murder weapon in here, I'm afraid." Hal caught the disappointed look on the inspector's face. "Sorry, Mike, these mallets are clean."

"Okay, Hal, thanks for coming out."

Soon the only people left in the shop were the two detectives. "I guess that's that," Bunyan said. "The murder weapon isn't in Grossman's shop after all."

The inspector frowned. "I was so sure." He studied the matter in silence.

"I guess we start over from scratch," the younger man said as the men headed for the exit and started walking slowly towards the cruiser in the parking lot.

"From scratch?" Mike repeated dully.

He focused intently and then … he knew!

"Get in," he said to his assistant as the two of them approached the squad car. "I'll give you a lift."

"Thanks, Boss." Paul made himself comfortable in the passenger seat.

They rode together in silence, each man lost in his own thoughts, until finally the cruiser came to a stop in front of a brick high rise in Toronto's Distillery District. Bunyan opened the car door and stepped out onto the sidewalk.

Watts leaned across the seat to give him some last minute instructions. "See you at 8 a.m. sharp tomorrow in my office, and listen, Paul, we're on the right track."

"Okay."

Paul closed the door behind him and started down the walkway towards his apartment complex when a thought suddenly occurred to him. He stopped abruptly.

Mike was just about to take off when he spotted his young protégé taking quick steps back towards the car.

"What's up?" he said, rolling down his window.

Paul crouched down beside the driver side door. "I was just thinking. How can you be so certain we're on the right track?"

"That's easy." Mike shifted into drive. "Hal's blue light. Like the man said—the LED doesn't lie."

WEDNESDAY
CHAPTER 24
SHOP TALK, PART 1

8:00 a.m.

Watts pulled the unwieldy whiteboard into the middle of the room and stood in front of it facing Bunyan who had planted himself on top of the inspector's desk.

"Let's examine each of the suspects in this case," he said, filling his and Bunyan's cups with coffee from the carafe in his office. "What we need to consider are three things: motive, opportunity, and alibi." Each word was then carefully written at the top of the board and underlined heavily.

Paul had his clipboard at the ready. "Who's first?" he asked, lifting a cup of coffee to his lips. He took a sip and grimaced.

"Gotta lower your standards, my boy," Watts smiled. "Now down to business. Let's start with the math teacher, Elaine Richardson," he said, dutifully writing her name down.

"Well," Paul remarked, "it was odd to find her coaster inside Principal Morris's office. The question is how did it get there?"

"Velma put it there," Watts said abstractedly stirring his coffee. "We had a little chat while you were scouting out the D'Agosta apartment building."

"Velma!? How did she get it?"

"Dino gave it to her to hold in safekeeping."

"And she agreed?!"

"Seems she was 'in love,' or as she herself put it 'they were having a fine romance.'"

"That woman really likes to play with fire, doesn't she?"

Watts shrugged.

"Do you think Mrs. Richardson knew about Velma's part in hiding her coaster?"

"I think she suspected, but couldn't be sure."

"Well, if the math teacher is our killer," Paul said, thinking out loud, "what do you suppose her motive might be?"

"Two possibilities come to mind," Mike paused to sip his coffee. "If she were infatuated with the boy and became aware of his other 'love interests,' she might have become enraged with jealousy. Or if, as the V.P. confided to me earlier, Dino intended to use the coaster as collateral for marks, then the motive becomes blackmail."

Paul considered the inspector's comments. "Okay, aside from a motive, do you think she had the opportunity?"

"Frankly, I think they all had the opportunity. Every suspect was in the parking lot the morning of the murder. They either drove there themselves or, in the case of Miss Malinsky, were dropped off there. And they all were in the area between 6 and 8 am. We can't eliminate anyone.

"Now as for Mrs. Richardson, it wouldn't have been that difficult for her to follow Dino into the field after he strayed there."

"I thought the pathologist said that Dino was lower than his assailant at the time of his murder. At six two he would have been quite a bit taller than his math teacher," Paul commented.

"I know," Watts agreed. "It is just possible that the kid had bent down to pick up something he dropped. Or maybe he was dazed from a blow he had received earlier. Either way, it would have presented the perfect opportunity for the woman to conk him on the head while he was in a vulnerable position."

Paul looked a bit doubtful. "Sure Mrs. Richardson may have had both the motive and the opportunity," he said, "but to me, the question remains. Does she have the temperament to be a killer?"

Watts turned the question over in his mind. "I've been a cop for over three decades, my boy, and I've come to one conclusion."

"Which is…?"

"Anyone is capable of anything."

Paul wasn't altogether convinced that the inspector was correct. "Well, I'll definitely keep an open mind. So, who's next on our list of suspects?"

"Let's have a look at the school's VP, Ms. Velma Vorchek."

"Your favorite." Paul grinned mischievously.

"Uh-huh. Believe it or not, the woman actually admitted to me that she was *addicted* to Dino. That might have prompted her to kill him in order to be free. Addicts can be dangerous."

"They were having an affair?" Paul asked incredulously. "Wouldn't that jeopardize her position with the board?"

"You just added another motive for murder."

"Do you think she was in the parking lot around the time the boy was killed?"

"Most likely, but I'll check on it further."

Paul shook his head in amazement. "That kid really got around. I'm surprised he had that much—energy."

"You have to remember he was seventeen years old and horny as hell—not to mention an unqualified sociopath."

"I agree. So, who's next?"

"Let's look at Julie Gauvin, the English teacher."

"We don't know much about her."

"That's right," Watts agreed. "She was very evasive the day we spoke to her. She's hiding *something*, I'm sure of it."

"Okay, so she's a 'maybe' for now. Who's next?"

"Armand Saint-Yves, the French teacher."

"What do you think of him," Paul asked curiously.

"It's quite possible he was another one of Dino's devoted 'fans.' That bullshit about the boy being like a 'priceless work of art' is wonky. The guy is nothing if not weird."

"Yes, but is he a killer?"

Watts gave the matter some thought. "Hard to say. Mr. Saint-Yves is basically an actor. People like him are never what they seem. Also, his classroom was located beside the parking lot, so he had proximity to the victim."

"Interesting. Like you, I believe he has something to hide, but is it something sinister or simply something a bit eccentric, like the man himself?"

"One way or another, we're going to find out," Watts said, pausing to down what was left in his cup. "Let's continue with the list of suspects, shall we? What did you make of Gunther Grossman?"

"If he thinks my name suits me," Paul said archly, "it's a case of the pot calling the kettle black."

Student Body

"Let's not get personal. Remember this, my boy, we're dealing with murder and the answer to who committed the crime will lie in the details. Now, let's get back to the shop teacher; he had opportunity, being in the vicinity; and he admitted that he hated Dino. The question is why? A teacher might be annoyed with a student who constantly skips class or even with one who gets mouthy now and then. But *hate* him… and so forcefully? I don't think so."

"So the man has something to hide?"

"Of course, he does. Just like the rest of the suspects. This murder was a crime of passion—look at the way the boy was killed. That kind of red hot rage is the result of enflamed emotions which could apply to all the suspects, including the last person on our list. Miss Malinsky."

"The science teacher?" Paul scratched his head. "Frankly she struck me as too cool to lose control. What makes her a suspect?"

"That walking stick of hers. We can't discount the fact that it's made out of rosewood—the same kind of wood found in microscopic fibers taken from the skull of the D'Agosta boy. That definitely makes her a potential suspect. Granted, she expressed nothing stronger than a disdain for the boy, but is she to be believed? A single, middle aged woman may very well have been flattered by the attentions of an attractive young male. Sometimes a dormant passion is aroused in a seemingly stable individual, and it might just push them over the edge. The result can be catastrophic."

"Oh come on," Bunyan scoffed, "you can't be serious. People don't kill someone simply because he turned them on. That's hardly a motive for murder."

"It's not that simple, my boy. The real victim—the one the killer actually wants to get rid of—is himself," Watts patiently explained. "When a powerful emotion gets stirred up, some people simply can't handle it. It's too overwhelming. In my time, I've seen people who tried to kill that part of themselves that they couldn't accept by committing acts of murder. Trust me, it happens."

"Okay, so our lonely spinster decides to kill her subconscious need for a man by bashing the boy on the back of his head with her walking stick? Is that what you're telling me?" Paul shook his head in disbelief.

"Remember what you said earlier about keeping an open mind."

"All right," Bunyan said thoughtfully. "I suppose it's possible to kill someone who puts you in touch with your vulnerable side." He threw his hands up the air. "Honestly, it's a sick world!"

Mike shrugged. "If it weren't, we'd be out of a job."

Paul grinned in spite of himself.

CHAPTER 25
JULIE GAUVIN

10:25 a.m.

Period Two had just ended, and the young English teacher sat at her desk watching as the last student filed out the door. Finally the room was empty, and Julie Gauvin was free to head out for a much needed break. But that wasn't happening. Instead, she remained where she was, rooted to her chair and staring off into space.

The only thing she knew with any certainty was that she was tired—more tired than she could remember being since the loss of her beloved mother.

If only she could get some sleep. Night after night, she lay in her bed exhausted until finally she fell into a fitful sleep that was laced with the same disturbing dream. There was Dino rushing towards her, clasping her shoulders in an iron-like grip and thrusting his erection against her groin. Every morning she woke up with her bed sheets drenched in sweat.

But nightmares were the least of her worries. Hanging over her head like the proverbial ax was the threat of discovery. And the worst part was she had to face this fear alone.

Now in her empty classroom with only her thoughts for company, she felt like she was about to lose her mind. She had to do something—*anything*—or she would go mad. Maybe if she walked over to the small staff room and poured herself a cup of coffee, she would feel better. Sometimes doing something seemingly normal can make a person believe that everything *is* normal. Then again, living in a fantasy world could prove risky. One only had to look at what it did to Dino to see that.

Somewhat dejected, Julie used the side of her hand to slide her assortment of magic markers into the top drawer of her desk when the sound of knocking made her jump. *Damn.* The last thing she wanted to do was engage in casual conversation with an eager student. But when she opened the portable door, she saw it wasn't a student.

"Miss Gauvin," Inspector Watts said politely, "we'd like a moment of your time."

"Of course," she said, backing up slightly. "Come in. Let's go sit at the front of the room… ah, do you think I should lock the door?" she asked apprehensively.

"Might be a good idea, Miss." Paul smiled to put her at ease.

"When we spoke to you yesterday in the parking lot," Watts began as soon as the three of them were seated, "you mentioned that you normally arrive at school each day around six thirty, at which time it is still dark outside. Is that correct?"

"Yes, Inspector."

"So, it's possible that anyone in the area could have seen the light coming from your window and known that you were in here?"

"Yes, that's right," she said, forcing her voice to stay steady.

"And students familiar with your policy of allowing them to enter your room beginning at 7:45 could have assumed that you would be alone in here prior to that time. Is *that* correct?"

"Yes," she answered warily. She concentrated on appearing natural, but every instinct told her to make a run for it.

"And you weren't afraid?"

Julie hesitated. She had this sinking feeling that one wrong answer would send her plummeting over a cliff. "No," she said in barely a whisper.

"Don't you think it would have better for you if you had been?" Watts asked quietly.

Julie was stunned. She retreated into the safety of silence.

Watts studied the young woman nervously avoiding his gaze.

"I'd like to suggest a certain scenario for you to consider, Miss Gauvin. On the morning of the murder you arrive at your usual time, 6:25 am and turn the light on in your portable. It's snowing heavily, and no one seems to be around."

Julie's throat tightened.

"As I was saying," the inspector continued, "Dino realizes you are not only alone but also in an isolated portable far from the main building. This is his chance. He's been successful with other staff members, so why wouldn't he be with you—someone much closer to his own age?"

Julie closed her eyes tightly to stifle the onset of tears. The detectives were watching her closely.

"So he approached you with all the confidence of a boy emboldened by his previous experiences. But this time he met resistance. Isn't that so, Miss Gauvin? This time he went too far, and you were frightened. So you fought back as hard as you could."

Julie buried her face in her hands. She felt like she was being sucked into a black hole from which there was no escape.

"You know, Miss Gauvin, that's what we *believe* happened," said the inspector. "Now here's what we *know*—so far. When the boy's body was taken to the forensic lab at police headquarters, there was a small wound, concave in shape, on his left temple. The force used to make this wound was delivered by a person who appeared to be determined but who lacked the kind of physical strength that would do significant damage. That led us to speculate that the wound was probably inflicted by a female trying to ward off the unwanted advances of an assailant. Does that make sense, Miss Gauvin?"

Julie opened her mouth to speak, but no words came out. Panic had paralyzed her.

Paul sensed that she was on the verge of collapse and stepped in. "We want to help you, Miss Gauvin. The wound on the temple didn't kill the boy. It was most likely the result of a person acting in self-defense." His voice was kind—pleading. "Is that what happened… Julie?"

The two detectives gave her a moment to consider. When she didn't respond, Watts began to speak, this time in a more intimidating tone.

"You know, Miss Gauvin, if the small wound on the side of the head wasn't the result of self-defense, the Crown prosecutor could make the case that you used the first blow to disable the boy, and after he left your classroom, you followed him across the parking lot into the empty field. Then, when he stumbled and fell to his knees, you delivered the fatal blow."

Julie tried to speak, but the words got stuck in her throat.

Watts continued, his voice firm. "Murder is serious business, Miss Gauvin. If the Crown could prove a case against you, you could be saying goodbye to your career. In fact, you could be saying goodbye to everything you care about, including your freedom, while you spend the remainder of your young life behind bars. Is that a chance you're willing to take?"

Julie burst into tears.

"Isn't it time you told us the truth?" Paul prodded gently.

Julie grabbed a handful of Kleenex from a box on her desk and continued crying quietly. After a while she blew her nose and struggled to compose herself.

Slowly she began recounting the events as they happened on the morning of the murder, stopping now and then to dab her eyes with soggy tissues. Finally, she explained that her intention was to report the incident later that same day, but the news of a body being found on school property stopped her cold. When she learned that the body belonged to Dino, terror seized her. She thought she might have killed him.

The inspector took a moment to reflect on her story.

"Do you still have the snow globe?" he asked finally.

Julie opened the bottom drawer and pulled out the cherished souvenir and held it in her open palm.

Watts retrieved a small plastic bag from his inside pocket and deposited the snow globe in it.

"Thank you, Miss Gauvin."

He nodded to Paul. The shape of the snow globe fit the description of the wound on the dead boy's temple.

"On your way to the main building after your encounter with Dino, did you see anyone?"

"The snow was coming down so heavily, and I was desperate to get back to my class before students started arriving, I hardly noticed a soul that morning."

The inspector was thoughtful for a moment. "Miss Gauvin," he said somberly, "have you spoken to *anyone* about what you have just told us?"

"No. I was too afraid. I didn't even confide in my dad who lives in Montreal." She began wringing her hands. "I just didn't know what to do. It has been such a burden—keeping this terrible secret."

"I understand." Watts conferred quietly with his partner before facing her again. "Miss Gauvin, it is imperative that you not tell anyone about what happened the morning of the murder. Do I have your promise?" He looked earnestly at her.

She seemed surprised by the intensity in his voice. "Of course, Inspector," she said. "But why the need for such secrecy?"

The expression on his face was grave. "You need to be clear about something, Miss Gauvin. Somebody at this school is a killer, and that person is extremely dangerous. The less the killer knows about your involvement with Dino, the safer you will be."

She took a deep breath. There was nothing for it now except to face the uncertain future with a steely resolve. "Is there anything I can do, Inspector?"

Paul was the one to answer her question with a reassuring smile. "Carry on as though nothing out of the ordinary has happened. Can you do that?"

"You can count on me," she said, straightening her shoulders.

Paul took her small hand in his and held it gently. "You're a brave girl, Julie Gauvin," he said softly. "A very brave girl, indeed."

CHAPTER 26
CHECKMATE

11:15 a.m.

The door to Velma's private office was already open when the two detectives walked in unannounced. The VP looked up from her desk.

"You again?" she said in a voice that could cut glass.

"Nice to see you too," Watts replied drolly.

"What can I do for you *this time*, Inspector?"

"You can get on the P.A. and announce there will be a meeting today at 4:00 in the small staffroom for those teachers whose names appear here." He handed her a list of names. "I expect you to be there too, Ms. Vorchek."

"I'm *not* a teacher here," she bristled.

"No, but based on our earlier conversation, it's clear you have had dealings with the victim that could prove important to solving this case."

She glared at him. "That was confidential information."

"And as I told you before, your secret will remain a secret as long as justice is not impeded," he said. "Now—back to your making the announcement…"

"You really do like to throw your weight around, don't you?"

"Just doing my job—like you do yours," he said.

She looked off into the distance as if searching for some sort of retort that would put this pompous ass in his place. "And just when am I supposed to make this big announcement?"

"Now would be a good time."

She stood up sharply. "Don't you ever get tired of giving orders?" she asked as she moved around her desk and headed for the door to the outer office.

The inspector eyed her coolly. "Do you?"

Paul resisted the urge to chuckle as he fell in behind the two of them filing out the door. Poor Velma Vorchek, going one-on-one with Mike Watts. He almost felt sorry for her.

CHAPTER 27
SHOP TALK, PART II

12:20 p.m.

Back at police headquarters, Watts and Bunyan were seated on opposite sides of the inspector's desk, unwrapping their Big Macs and carefully prying lids off steaming cups of coffee.

They were both in a good mood and for good reason—the investigation was going well. They had several viable suspects and a few strong leads. Each man was confident that it was only a matter of time before they solved the D'Agosta case. All they needed now was the kind of hard evidence that would stand up in court, and Watts was already mentally sifting through strategies that would make that happen.

He took a sip of coffee and furrowed his brow. "Did you manage to trace the jewelry store from the imprinting on the bottom of the box?" he asked, wiping his mouth with a handful of serviettes.

"Yes," Paul replied. "After some digging, I narrowed it down to the Peoples store at the Cloverdale Mall in Etobicoke. I'll be going there this afternoon to check it out."

"Good. Of course, the whole thing may be innocent—relatively speaking. On the other hand, it could point to an incriminating level of involvement with the murder victim. One way or another, we'll find out the truth."

He stopped to take a bite of his burger. "The Cloverdale Mall, huh? I've been there once or twice—mostly to buy socks—but I never noticed it had a jewelry store. I guess an old bachelor like me has no need for that kind of stuff."

"No, I guess not," Bunyan said wistfully.

Watts hesitated. It seemed like a good time to take a sip of coffee which was now cool enough to drink. "Have you been to Peoples before?" he asked casually, "maybe to price out rings for that girlfriend of yours?"

Paul crumpled up the white bag that had contained his lunch and tossed it in the trash. He seemed to be more silent than usual, and when he finally did speak, his voice was listless—as if it belonged to somebody else and not to him.

"I *used* to have a girlfriend," he said. "But a few months ago she dumped me." He paused to shake himself slightly as if sadness didn't sit well with his sunny disposition. "It doesn't help to dwell on it," he said, staring vacantly out the window.

Mike gave him an enquiring look but did not pursue the subject. Paul was a deeply private person, and if he had decided not to open up, that was his prerogative. A man has to deal with disappointments in his own way.

Paul picked up one of the serviettes and began rolling it in his hand until it became as round and solid as a marble. "It was good at first," he said. "We had a charming little flat in the Bloor West Village close to the European bakeries and butcher shops we both love. But then, after a while, she started getting restless." He closed his eyes as if to block out the pictures in his mind.

"Apparently, or so she said, our relationship wasn't what she had envisioned when we met," he said focusing inward. "It seemed what she wanted was someone who would come home every night after work and *be* with her. I couldn't do that. I am a law enforcement officer, and that means being on call 24/7. She said she could never make plans, and that I wasn't really committed to the relationship.

"After a while she actually seemed to *resent* my job. I tried to tell her that police work is demanding but that there was still room in my life for her," he said, strain showing in his voice. "She said that just wasn't good enough, and then one night she packed her bags and called a cab. What could I do but say goodbye and wish her well." He shrugged and looked away.

Mike mulled the matter over in his mind. "Well, my boy," he said, "obviously that wasn't the woman for you." He paused to find the right words. "Being involved with a cop is never easy. The hours are long, and the work can be dangerous. You often don't discover that you're with someone who can't handle it until they walk out the door, leaving you with a broken heart."

He cleared his throat. "Many decades ago, when I was about your age and starting out on the force, I made a decision. I knew marriage would be a major distraction to my work, and I wanted to keep my mind clear and my life uncomplicated so I could concentrate on being a cop. That lifestyle worked for me, but that doesn't mean it's right for everybody. We all make choices, and then we have to stick by them."

He had an idea. "You know, my boy, teachers are just naturally bossy—they can't help themselves. They're wired that way. But some of them are worth the trouble. Plus they earn a big buck and get all that time off. Shack up with one of them, and you could go hiking in the Rockies all summer if you felt like it."

Paul looked surprised. "A teacher, huh? Even if she turned out to be a killer?"

"Look, all I'm saying is think about it."

Paul didn't know how to respond. All this fatherly advice coming from the man who was his boss was confusing, and yet, somehow, endearing. He decided to change the subject.

"I'm on my way to the mall right now. Got any plans of your own?"

"You bet. I'm off to pay a little visit to the board of education. There are some records of employment I want to take a look at before the staff meeting today. My hunch is there's a lot of dirty laundry buried somewhere in those files."

"Shall we meet back here at three to compare notes?"

"That's not enough time for me to make it back to the school. Let's make it 3:30 in the Fairmont parking lot. We can share information in the squad car before we head into the building."

"Right, Boss." Bunyan started to get up. "It should be an interesting meeting. What's our agenda?"

"Basically we need to coax the whole story out of some of the suspects who are holding out on us, and after that, we're going to need a lot of patience and a little bit of luck."

"Luck? That's not what we learned at the academy," he said wryly.

Mike had a crafty look on his face.

"Paul, my boy, I've been a cop since before you were born, and in all that time I've learned a simple truth. Not one of us would make it through the day without a little bit of luck."

CHAPTER 28
SETTING THE STAGE

4:00 p.m.

The bulky staffroom furniture had been shoved against the wall, and five folding chairs had been arranged in a row facing the door. The first teachers to arrive were Magda Malinsky and Julie Gauvin.

"I don't know why we have to go through this again," Magda grumbled, using her walking stick for support as she lowered herself onto the hard metal chair. "You'd think the cops would have enough information by now to make an arrest and get this thing over with."

"Oh, for god's sake, Magda, don't be so callous," Julie snapped. "A boy was murdered. Sitting through another staff meeting seems like a trifle compared to that."

Magda turned to stare at her. It wasn't like Julie to be so short tempered. Something was wrong. She had no idea what that something was, but Magda's instincts told her it was a good time to keep her mouth shut—and her eyes and ears open.

Julie herself was worried about her outburst. Up to now she hadn't appreciated how much her nerves were on edge. Obviously she couldn't trust herself not to say something she might later regret, so she withdrew into silence. But her thoughts weren't silent. If anything, they were driving her crazy. Her mind kept going over things she had said to the two detectives that morning. Did they believe that she had acted in self-defense? Or did they suspect she trailed Dino into the empty field and then killed him?

Why did she tell them about the snow globe? Now that they had it in their possession, what were they going to do with it? Could whatever evidence remained on the glass surface prove her undoing?

And why another staff meeting *now*? The inspector had something up his sleeve, she was sure of it. Would it turn out to be something that would implicate her?

If only she had someone she could trust. If only she could stop this endless cycle of worrisome mind chatter. If only…

"Saving this seat for me?" Gunther grinned down at her. Before Julie could come up with a response, he had already parked himself in the chair beside hers. "Man, it's cold outside," he said turning to face her. "You don't mind if I warm myself up next to you" he said, nudging her playfully with his forearm.

Julie's eyes widened in comic disbelief. Then she started to laugh. And she couldn't stop. When she finally caught her breath, she realized she was actually grateful to Gunther. His silly schoolboy attempt at flirting had her laughing so hard, she was able to relax for the first time in days.

"I don't know what's so funny, Julie," Armand sniffed, as he scurried past her. "I should think you would want to show a little more decorum under the circumstances. We're all under suspicion in the death of poor Dino, and the police aren't about to give up trying to pin the rap on one of us." He sat down stiffly at the far end of the row, leaving two empty chairs between himself and Gunther.

Elaine Richardson entered the staff room next and immediately spotted the remaining empty chairs. She had to choose to sit beside either Gunther or Armand. She chose Armand.

At the front of the room close to the door, Velma Vorchek was leaning against the wall with her arms crossed tightly. Her expression was grim, as if she was about to launch into a lecture reprimanding the staff for some unknown misdemeanor. But she wasn't the one who had called the meeting, and she wasn't the one calling the shots. In fact, that was the real reason for the pained expression on her face.

A few moments later, Inspector Mike Watts entered the staffroom followed by his ever present partner.

Velma moved to the only vacant spot left and sat down between Gunther and Elaine. Originally she had planned to remain standing at the front of the room to let everyone

Student Body

know she was still in charge, but then she changed her mind. If she were seated, she could study the inspector's face as he was speaking. It might reveal more than his words would.

"Thank you for coming," the inspector said, in a precise voice. "The purpose of this meeting is to discuss certain facts surrounding the murder of a student here at this school."

An uneasy stir filled the room.

"First of all, no crime exists in isolation. There is always a background, often obscured somewhere in the shadows. To that end, I made a trip to the board office this afternoon, where I, indeed, discovered information critical to this case. For the moment that information will remain confidential while the police do a thorough investigation of all the parties involved." He stared meaningfully at the teachers, one by one. "Consider that fair warning," he said.

Watts detected an inrush of breath.

"I will now be talking about the murder victim, DiAngelo D'Agosta. This was no ordinary student. There is ample evidence to support the fact that he used extortion or seduction to get what he wanted—whether it was a credit in a course, an unearned mark, or the expensive jewelry we discovered in his mother's apartment. Each of these 'benefits' presents a perfect motive for murder.

The room remained silent.

"Then there was the odd situation of a missing coaster that belonged in a private home and ended up in the office of the school's absent principal. This episode smacks of collusion and blackmail, and, once again, speaks to a motive for murder. On the other hand, blackmail doesn't necessarily lead to murder.

"The fact is that Dino liked to play games—very dangerous games. He liked pulling strings like a puppet master, and he was an expert at homing in on a person's particular vulnerability. At this point, we know the names of the parties involved in the case of the missing coaster. What is not so certain is the consequence of Dino's attempt at blackmail. But we *will* find out.

"And now, lastly, I will be addressing the issue of the murder weapon. Our forensic unit was here on the morning of the murder and combed the area around the portables, including the field next to the parking lot and the dumpsters next to the shop portable. Since that time, we have come to the conclusion that the murder weapon most likely was *inside* one of the portables and not on the grounds surrounding them. Therefore, our forensic unit will be returning to Fairmont tomorrow morning at 7:00 am to conduct a thorough examination inside each of the portable classrooms—the shop portable in particular.

"Each person in this room is requested to be back here tomorrow afternoon at 4:00 pm when the results of this search will be revealed."

No one moved a muscle.

Student Body

"Finally, I want to say this. All the evidence indicates that the murder victim, DiAngelo D'Agosta, was a nasty piece of work. He had no compunction about taking advantage of anyone who could advance his cause, and he never took 'no' for an answer. His specialty was seducing people—it didn't matter to him if his target was male or female. His top priority was to achieve his goal. Nevertheless, he is entitled to justice, and you can be assured that we will nail whoever killed this kid. That is all. You may go."

Stunned by the curt dismissal, people got up without a word and made their way towards the door. When the room had emptied, Bunyan came over and stood beside his partner.

"That was some speech," he said archly. "My guess is there will be quite a fallout."

"That's the idea." Watts smiled cagily.

CHAPTER 29
DRAGON LADY

5:15 p.m.

The meeting was over and Bunyan and Watts were in the rear foyer of the school preparing to leave when Paul noticed that the staff inspector was lagging a few feet behind. "You coming?" he said, turning around.

"No. You go on ahead. There's something I need to discuss with Ms. Vorchek."

"You mean about the—"

"Go home," said Watts. "Try to get a few hours' sleep. You're going to need it."

"Still picking me up at midnight?"

"Check! Now, off with you!"

—

Student Body

Following the staff meeting Velma Vorchek had returned to her office and sat glumly behind her desk, thinking. When Principal Morris went on sick leave and left the school in her hands, she thought she'd *arrived*. Finally she had the authority she'd always craved. This was *her* school, these teachers were *her* staff. She could rewrite rules, change school policy, hire and fire at will—basically do anything she wanted. And no one *dared* stand in her way. It was a dream come true.

And then there was this boy—this irresistible boy—leading her into a thicket filled with thorns for which she was not prepared. She had thought she could handle him, thought she could take what she wanted and walk away whenever she felt like it. It was going to be great.

If only it had turned out that way!

—

It was dark outside, and everyone had gone home. Staring at the pile of papers on her desk, Velma had two choices—stay where she was and immerse herself in bureaucratic bullshit or go home to an empty house. She was about to choose the latter when she sensed someone at her door.

"Excuse me." The inspector rapped lightly on her door before pushing it open. "I see you're packing up to go," he said, approaching her desk. "I'll only keep you a minute."

Velma closed her briefcase and fastened the snaps before looking up. "Got something on your mind, Inspector? Seems to me you covered just about everything in the staff meeting."

"Not quite everything." He pulled up a chair next to her desk. "You recall at our last meeting that you practically begged me to keep your secret life—*secret*?"

Velma eyed him warily. "Yes."

"Well, I thought we might have a discussion about that here in the privacy of your office."

Velma's straightened up. "Okay, Inspector." Her voice was tinged with tiredness and resentment. "You're here to tell me something. What is it?"

"You tell me, Ms. Vorchek."

Velma sighed. "It's about those gold chains you found in Dino's mother's apartment, isn't it?"

"Are you ready to confess?"

"I confess that I bought gold chains for him. But I won't confess to murder. I didn't kill Dino." She turned her face away. "I loved him," she said in a small voice.

"We have proof that you bought the boy jewelry. Now, do you want to change your story, while you still can?"

"Inspector," she said firmly, "I did not kill Dino D'Agosta. Yes, I did give him a set of gold chains, and yes, I did have an affair with him. I know it sounds bad, and I'm not particularly proud of how I behaved, but as I once told you, I would have done anything for him."

"As I recall, you said he was like a drug."

Velma cast her eyes down. Yes. He was a drug for me," she said sadly. "But I swear to you, I didn't kill him."

"Let's assume that is true, Ms. Vorchek. What do you know about the people arriving in the teacher parking lot the morning Dino was murdered?"

"I don't know any more than you do. I wish I did," she added softly.

"You saw nothing suspicious when you parked your car that morning?"

"Nothing out of the ordinary. In fact, nothing at all through the heavy snowfall."

"I see." He stared at her. "Ms. Vorchek, I found a link at the school board this afternoon that provides solid proof of your complicity in the corruption of a minor prior to your transfer to this school."

Velma inhaled deeply. "Yes," she said quietly. "What do you want from me?"

"I want your assurance that you will not withhold any more pertinent information related to this murder investigation?"

"Yes, of course, Inspector." She paused nervously. "Are you going to arrest me?"

"Not today," he said, going out the door.

CHAPTER 30
SMOKE AND MIRRORS

8:00 p.m.

Velma Vorchek parked her car in the designated area of her townhouse complex and wearily headed for her unit at the end of the building. She inserted the key in her ground-level front door and pushed it open with her free hand. The mail, which had been shoved through the slot in the door earlier in the day, lay scattered at her feet. She picked up the lot and, after a cursory glance through it, stuffed all of it into the wire holder hanging on the wall beside her key rack. The mail could wait.

Slipping out of her coat, she tossed it casually onto the entryway bench. Actually the word entryway was a bit of a misnomer; there was no formal *entryway*. The front door opened immediately into Velma's living room, and the bench had been conveniently placed beside it. Of course, the setup wasn't ideal, but since it was cost effective to live in the townhouse she had gotten in her divorce settlement, it would have to do for the time being.

Student Body

Velma rested for a few seconds on the bench to pull off her boots, a pair of fashionable Cougar Cheyenne's that fit her shapely calves like a second skin. She reached down to grasp one boot at a time and tugged as hard as she could. In her stocking feet, she leaned back against the wall and closed her eyes.

Finally she could turn her mind to things that had nothing to do with that soul-sucking beast, Fairmont Fucking High. She inhaled deeply and started making a mental list of how she might spend her evening. First, she would have a nice, long bubble bath—she had always found that relaxing. Then, maybe, she'd make a meal out of Godiva chocolates. What was to stop her? On the other hand, she might just get up, march right over to her liquor cabinet, and proceed to drink herself into a stupor. Now there was a tantalizing idea!

God. She was tired.

Tired of petty details piling up on her desk day after day. Tired of spoiled, overpaid teachers who bitched endlessly. Tired of rude, snarky students who sneered at authority. Tired. Tired. Tired.

And then there was that other thing! That murder thing!!

Dino fucking D'Agosta! Was he ever going to go away? That damn boy was causing as much trouble in death as he had in life!

Well, she had had enough. It was time to unwind. She made an executive decision. First, she would have a leisurely soak in the tub, and then maybe stretch out on the sofa and watch some mindless TV. She started unbuttoning her blouse while heading for the bathroom. The ringing of the doorbell stopped her in her tracks.

—

"What are you doing here?!"

"Is that any way to greet a fella?" Gunther was leaning against her doorway, a bottle of Chardonnay in his hand, a wicked smile on his face.

"Go home," she said bluntly. "The shop is closed."

He laughed. "Aw, c'mon, Princess. You know you don't want to be alone tonight." He gave her a coy look.

Velma sighed. He was right. A part of her *didn't* want to be alone, but she wasn't about to admit it. Men! Sometimes they had this uncanny way of getting inside a woman's head.

She hesitated.

"I can't stay out here all night," he said teasingly. "We really need to get this wine on ice."

Without saying a word, Velma turned and trotted back into her living room. Gunther followed, shedding his overcoat on the entryway bench and dropping down beside it.

"So," he asked, kicking off his waterproof slip-ons. "Are we going out… or ordering in?"

"There's the phone," she gestured towards the front hall.

Gunther chuckled. "Chinese?"

"Sure," she said, collapsing on the couch. Actually, some spring rolls and a nice cold glass of Chardonnay sounded pretty good.

"Let's have a toast while we're waiting for the food to arrive," he suggested on his way to the kitchen to retrieve wine glasses.

"A toast? Are you kidding?!" Velma sat up straight, anger giving her a shot of adrenaline. "What on earth is there to toast? Being suspects in a murder case? Having innuendos and threats thrown in our faces by that pompous ass running the show? Just what is it *exactly* we have to celebrate?"

Gunther sat down beside her and filled her glass. "Look at it this way, Princess. The Inspector may have 'thrown out a lot of innuendoes,' in the staff meeting, but just think about what he didn't say. *No* names were mentioned. *No* arrests were made. *No* one was singled out at any time before, during, or after the meeting." Gunther stopped to pour himself a drink. "You know what that means, don't you?" He settled back against the sofa cushion and swirled the wine around in his glass.

Velma had to admit she was more curious than annoyed. Sure, Gunther was full of himself most of the time, but he was also smart. It might be worth her while to hear what he had to say.

"Okay, Mr. Know-It-All, enlighten me."

"It means, my little nymphet that the police have diddly squat. Otherwise, why are they waiting to make an arrest? Figure it out. All that posturing today in the staff room, that was just smoke and mirrors. In any case I'm not worried," he said, studying his glass. "Are you?"

Velma turned her head in the direction of the front door. "I wonder when that food will get here. I'm starved."

He eyed her narrowly. "One thing the Inspector told us specifically was that he found out something at the school board office. Of course, he didn't say what that something is, but I'd bet the farm that *you* know."

"You're crazy," she said, turning away quickly.

"No, I'm not." Gunther set his wine glass down on the coffee table. "You're the one at Fairmont with board connections. You're the one with access to the employment records. You know what he was talking about. So tell me."

"What makes you think I'd give confidential information like that to you?"

"Why not?" he said, smiling slyly. "You gave it to Dino, didn't you?"

"What makes you think that?"

He reached for his glass of wine on the coffee table. "Well, first of all, you didn't deny it, and second of all, Dino sometimes shared things with me"

Student Body

A queasy feeling overcame her, but Velma willed it away. She could throw up later. Right now she needed answers, and she was going to get them. Snuggling up to him, she slipped her hand inside the front of his shirt.

"What kind of things?" she purred.

"Nothing specific. Just juicy generalities—mostly about you."

Velma was suddenly afraid. All this time she had thought she was the one with the upper hand, the one who knew all the secrets. But she was wrong. The person at Fairmont who'd been calling the shots was a seventeen-year-old boy who had skillfully played everyone, herself included.

The world was suddenly whirling around her. She raised a limp hand and held it against her forehead which was slick with sweat. Nausea was creeping up her throat.

"Are you all right?" Gunther looked genuinely concerned. "Can I get you something—a bicarbonate? Tylenol? Maybe some—"

Before he could finish his sentence, Velma jumped up and rushed out of the room, her hand clasped over her mouth. Gunther stared in astonishment. He was about to go after her when the doorbell rang. He stood up and reached into his back pocket for his wallet.

Gunther took the large paper bag from the delivery man's hand and paid the bill, including a generous tip. Then he spread the contents of small white boxes and little packets of plum and soy sauce around the coffee table.

"Velma, you should see this spread," he called out to her. "Come on back. A little food will settle your stomach. It always does for me."

When she didn't answer, he went looking for plates in the kitchen. In a little while Velma returned, looking grey and drawn.

"Gunther, I couldn't eat a thing," she said, falling into the big overstuffed chair opposite the sofa.

"But what about all this food?"

"Take it home with you," she said weakly.

Gunther shrugged. "Well, okay." He started repacking the large paper bag with the assorted boxes and various little plastic packets of sauce.

"I hate to leave you like this. You look like hell."

She managed a small smile. "I bet you say that to all the girls."

"Just the ones I want to sleep with," he said drolly. He paused to study her. "No, really, it seems a shame to leave you. You look like you need something…"

She stood up a bit wobbly and began shuffling towards the hallway leading to her bedroom.

Alone in Velma's living room, Gunther wondered if maybe he shouldn't follow her, but decided against it. Then, grabbing the bag containing the Chinese food, he quietly disappeared out the front door.

In her bedroom, Velma slipped into her favorite fuzzy slippers and soft chenille bathrobe. When she returned to the living room, Gunther was gone. It was just as well. She was dealing with a throbbing headache and a raw sore throat, so there was nothing left to do but go to bed. Alone.

She gathered up the wine glasses and the bottle of Chardonnay and headed for the kitchen. She had just put the wine back in the fridge and the glasses in the sink when, once again, the doorbell rang. Reluctantly she strolled into her living room but stopped before going further. She was in no mood to deal with any more interruptions, Gunther included, so she decided to pretend she had already gone to bed. She remained motionless as the minutes ticked by.

The doorbell rang again. This time she was annoyed. It should have been obvious to anyone that she didn't wish to be disturbed. Cinching her chenille robe tightly around her waist, she stomped angrily to the front door, flipped on the porch light, and stepped out onto the landing.

There on the front porch was a single long stem American Beauty rose inside a slender milk white vase. Gunther must have made arrangements earlier in the day to have it sent to her home address. It was just like him to surprise her by doing something unexpectedly sweet. The rose was one of the most beautiful she had ever seen.

Holding her hand to her heart, she bent down to pick it up.

Bev Bachmann

The blow was swift and sudden. Within seconds Velma lay in a crumbled heap on her welcome mat like a broken doll some petulant child had gotten tired of playing with.

CHAPTER 31
"THEY SHOULD HAVE BEEN THERE."

10:05 p.m.

Eager to get back to his office, Watts sped up the stone stairs of police headquarters two at a time. The moment he stepped through the door, he knew from the look on Bunyan's face something was seriously wrong.

"What happened?"

"There was an emergency call to an address in Swansea." He paused soberly. "It's Velma. She's been assaulted."

Watts looked grim. "Who made the 911 call?"

"A neighbor who was walking his dog. He noticed that the front light was on and the door was ajar. When he went in to investigate, he saw a woman sprawled on the living room floor. That's when he called 911."

"Is she still alive?"

"As far as I know. She's been transported to Toronto Western."

"What's the current status?"

"Uniformed officers are on the scene right now."

"Good!" Mike grabbed his coat and headed for the door. "Call the officer in charge and tell him to keep the witness there until we arrive. You can use the radio in the car. Let's go."

—

Police cars were parked up and down the street, their beacons flashing like merry-go-rounds on speed. A few neighbors had gathered in little clusters in front of Velma's house, gaping at the sight of police going in and out. They spoke softly to each other in subdued tones of curiosity mingled with compassion.

The two detectives dashed quickly past them and through the opened door into Velma's living room. Watts immediately approached the senior officer at the scene.

"It looks odd, Inspector," the officer said. "If the purpose of the visit was to attack the woman, then why do it outside instead of in the house where he wouldn't be seen?"

"She was attacked outside? How do you know?"

"We found blood stains on the welcome mat."

Watts went outside and bent down to get a closer look. He spotted the blood and a knocked over flower vase with a long stem red rose nearby.

Back inside the townhouse, he spoke again to the senior officer. "What do you make of it?"

"Based on the blood stains outside and where we found her when we arrived, I would say she was attacked outside and then dragged into the house."

"I think you're right about that," Watts agreed. "Why do you suppose he didn't close the door completely?"

"Haste? Fear? Forgetfulness? Could be any number of reasons. I suspect the perpetrator was focused on getting in and out quickly."

Mike nodded.

"Did you get any information from the paramedics before they left for the hospital?"

"They were pretty busy, but I did overhear one of them say the hair on the back of her head was matted with blood. She was unconscious when they put her in the ambulance."

The senior officer looked around the interior and shook his head. "I tell you, Inspector, I'm skeptical. I doubt the state of this room was caused by an argument that got out of hand. I mean, take a good look around," he said with a wave of his hand. "See if you come to the same conclusion."

Watts's eyes swept over the scene. Sofa cushions were strewn about the floor, a glass shelving unit had been overturned and shards were everywhere. The officer was right. It just didn't add up.

"It's just plain weird," the officer continued. "If the assailant's intention was to harm the victim, why attack the furniture? None of it makes any sense—unless the two of them struggled around the living room, and he caught up with her when she ran outside. Forensics will be able to tell us if there are any defensive wounds on the victim, but I didn't see any myself. Frankly, I think the woman was taken by surprise."

Watts tended to agree but needed more information. "Was there any damage to the rest of the house?"

"No. Just what you see here."

"And you're sure nothing is missing?"

"Well, we found the victim's purse upside down on the floor by a pair of leather boots. Her cash and credit cards were intact. If robbery was the motive, this was one sloppy burglar." "

"I think you're right," Mike agreed. "This scene has definitely been staged. Of course, we can't overlook the presence of the rose and the white vase," he said. "Looks to me like this crime wasn't random. I'd say she was set up."

"Excuse me." A small man in a plaid windbreaker stood tentatively in the kitchen doorway. "The officer in charge asked me to wait in here so I wouldn't be in the way, but I really need to get home," he said timidly. "My wife will be worried, and it's past Shasta's bedtime."

"Shasta?"

"That's my Papillion hiding under the table." Shasta came out at the sound of her name and looked up inquiringly with large luminous eyes.

Watts gave the little dog a bemused smile. "So that's Shasta, is it? And may I assume you are the person who called in the crime?"

"That's right. My name is Gaines. My wife and I live five houses down the street."

"Well, Mr. Gaines, I have only a few questions. What made you approach the townhouse?"

"Well, it was curious that the front light was on and the door was partially open, although that could have been for any number of reasons."

"And what made you go into the house?"

"It was Shasta," the man explained. "As I said, the light was on and the door was ajar, so I moved in closer to see if anything was wrong. Shasta immediately started sniffing intensely at the welcome mat. I bent down to see what she was sniffing at, and that's when I saw stains that looked like blood." Gaines looked queasy.

"And that's when you decided to enter the townhouse?" Watts prompted.

"Yes."

"What did you see when you came through the front door?"

"The place was a shambles. Obviously something terrible had happened here. It was shocking—especially when I spotted a woman lying motionless on the floor. I couldn't tell if she was alive or dead, I just knew I had to call 911 right away. After that, I took Shasta outside, and the two of us waited for help to arrive."

"You did the absolute right thing, Mr. Gaines. However, I'm going to ask you to agree to be fingerprinted. It's strictly voluntary on your part and will only take a few minutes. But it will help us to sort out the fingerprints that we find in here."

"Oh, Inspector, is that really necessary?" He seemed frightened. "I've never been in trouble with the law."

"It'll be fine," Watts said reassuringly. "If you like, we can do the fingerprinting at your house so your wife will know what has happened and that you and Shasta are safe—and not in any trouble with the law."

"I'd appreciate that" said Gaines as he started towards the door sandwiched between two officers with Shasta trotting behind them. Just before he reached the door the inspector called after him.

"You know, Mr. Gaines, your quick response to this emergency probably saved a woman's life tonight."

The man's eyes lit up. "Oh, I hope so," he said earnestly as he was escorted out the door. "I hope so."

"It's obvious the perpetrator of this crime was after something," Watts remarked to Bunyan after everyone had left.

Student Body

"We have to find out what that something is. I want you to look around the room as if you're taking photographs with your eyes. Try to figure out what you're not seeing because *something* is missing. Something important." "Right, Boss." Paul began a slow, methodical search. He took the covers off the sofa cushions and combed through the broken glass from the smashed shelving unit. Then he took paintings down and examined the walls behind them. He studied framed photos, looked behind drapes, got down on all fours and lifted up area rugs. Nothing.

Meanwhile Watts scrutinized the room himself, casting his gaze in a wide circle as if trying to get the big picture while Bunyan was focusing on the small details. His eyes drifted over to where Velma's boots had been strategically placed under the entryway bench where she had placed them earlier that evening. Then he shifted his gaze upwards to the wire mail holder hanging on the wall and the key rack beside it. He focused on this area with a look of fixed concentration. And then he knew.

"Paul," he said, waving him over. "Have a look at the area where Velma probably takes off her boots. What do you see?"

The young detective moved closer to the front door. Suddenly he frowned.

"It doesn't make any sense."

"What doesn't make sense, my boy?"

Paul ran his hand through his hair. "I can't believe I didn't see it. They should have been there."

"*What* should have been there?"

"Her keys," Paul said. "When a person is home, they don't need their keys unless they're going out."

Mike smiled. The boy was going to make one fine detective.

THURSDAY

CHAPTER 32: THE LONG NIGHT

12:25 a.m.

The sky was an oily shade of grey as if someone had tried to wipe it clean with a dirty rag. A half-moon cast murky shadows on the city sleeping below. It was the perfect night for a stakeout.

Mike checked his watch. It was still early.

Each man unscrewed the top of his thermos and filled his cup with strong black coffee. After that there was nothing to do but wait.

It was going to be a long night.

The thought flashed through Mike's mind that he might run the engine to get a bit of heat going inside the cab, but that would have been reckless. The last thing he wanted to do was alert the neighborhood to their presence. Besides, being warm and comfortable might induce a state of sleepiness and neither cop could afford that. They had to stay sharp, whatever the cost.

This was the first time these two detectives had worked a stakeout together, and it amazed Watts that his young partner was managing to hold up so well in the cold and mind numbing boredom. Maybe it was different with the younger generation. Their bodies hadn't yet been subjected to years of long nights, stale coffee, and constant stress. What's more, they had the stamina of youth on their side. But then again, Mike mused, maybe he was just making excuses for himself.

The hours ticked away in silence. The two detectives had decided early on not to talk—this wasn't a social occasion—but Watts did make a point earlier to fill his partner in on his plan for the evening, and that plan was far from simple. It required precise timing, infinite patience, and perhaps even, as he had mentioned once before, a little bit of luck. It all depended on the bait he had surreptitiously slipped into the staff meeting the previous day. Was it enticing enough to coax a killer out of hiding?

A cruel wind swirled in and out of century-old houses crammed side by side along the narrow street leading to Fairmont's parking lot. Two blocks away, the school stood solid as a sentry waiting for the morning to come and with it hundreds of kids eager to escape the domestic drudgery of their circumscribed lives. For some, education would turn out to be a head start to a promising future. For others it would be nothing more than the beginning of a series of dead ends. Fate and fortitude would be the deciding factors.

Student Body

Meanwhile the windshield had been fogging up. Paul kept the ice scraper busy dealing with it. The task was easy. His long arms rivaled those of an orangutan.

Mike took another sip of his now lukewarm coffee and glanced over his shoulder at the small contraption lying on the back seat. "You sure you know how to use that thing?"

"You mean the infrared camera?"

Watts nodded.

"Yeah, I do," Paul said, smiling to himself. He was up-to-date with new technology, and using an infrared camera was child's play to him. But Bunyan wasn't smug about it. In fact, he considered himself lucky to be working alongside a man with one of the sharpest minds in law enforcement. If Staff Inspector Mike Watts lagged a little behind in keeping up with technology—as was true of many of his generation—well, so be it.

They had been waiting since shortly after midnight, and now it was almost 4:30 a.m. If Mike was right, their quarry should be showing up at any minute. They didn't have long to wait.

CHAPTER 33
THE TRAP

7:10 a.m.

The heavy snowfall the day of the murder had obliterated all traces of footprints that might have held a clue; nevertheless, the forensic unit had returned to the area in the field where the body had been discovered, and they were now weaving their flashlights around in circular patterns on the snow packed ground. They stopped occasionally to inspect an item of interest before depositing it into a sterile bag with a zip-lock closure.

They had received instructions from Inspector Watts the day before to re-examine the crime scene for possible fresh evidence. He had been very specific about the time during which they were to arrive. It had to coincide with the hour he mentioned in the previous staff meeting. As well, he knew that 7:00 a.m. would give his team a clear field in which to work and yet be late enough that staff and students would start arriving and become members of a ready-made audience.

The inspector was certain that the killer would blend into the audience to observe the operations of the forensic team.

Out of sight in the shop portable, Bunyan and McCormick from the forensic unit had been meticulously going over all the tools used by the students and instructor and had, as per Watts's instructions, collected the wood carving kit kept in the shop portable.

As fading clouds shifted to make way for the stubborn sun, visibility became clearer by the moment, and everyone could see Paul come out of the shop portable. He turned and held the door open for Hal who proceeded down the portable steps, a large white Styrofoam container carefully balanced between his two hands.

"Okay, Mike, what do you want done with this?"

"Take it back to the lab and compare any blood found on the mallets with that of the victim."

McCormick furrowed his brow. "We've been over this area before, and all the mallets were clean. You sound like you expect a different result this time. Is there a reason for that?"

"Call it a hunch," Watts said wryly.

Hal shook his head. "This whole thing is odd, very odd," he commented casually while walking the short distance to the curb where the forensic van was parked. "If one of the mallets is, indeed, the murder weapon, then why would the killer not dispose of it or, at the very least, hide it somewhere safe and not leave it in a classroom where anyone could find it?"

"Who knows how a killer's mind works," Mike quipped.

"I thought maybe you might," Hal said, transferring his load to the van's cargo hold and then hoisting himself into the driver's seat. It was the signal for his team to climb in the back with their gear and buckle up.

Watts nodded his acknowledgement as their van slowly pulled away from the curb and slipped into the morning traffic

CHAPTER 34
HOUR OF RECKONING, PART I

4:00 p.m.

"Thank you all for being here. I know your workday has ended, and you're eager to be on your way. However, no one will be allowed to leave until the meeting is concluded." He reinforced his statement by directing their attention to the uniformed guard posted beside the room's only exit.

Those teachers who had been at the staff meeting the previous afternoon—Julie Gauvin, Magda Malinsky, Elaine Richardson, Armand Saint-Yves, and Gunther Grossman—were now once again seated directly in front of Staff Inspector Mike Watts.

This time there was no polite chit-chat, no nervous fidgeting, no angry grumblings. This time no one complained loudly that the meeting was yet another waste of time. Everyone knew that what they were about to hear could change the course of their lives.

"First of all," Watts said solemnly, "you will notice that one of you is missing. Last night Vice Principal Vorchek was attacked on the front porch of her house, and she is now in a hospital ICU ward, comatose but breathing on her own."

All that day rumors had been circulating about the VP's absence, but no one knew any details. So the news that she had been attacked shocked the people in the room.

Gunther started to say something, but quickly changed his mind. He had no idea if anyone had seen him in her house last night. However, if the police were to examine Velma's phone records and find that a call had been made to a Chinese restaurant, it wouldn't take them long to locate the delivery guy who could identify him. What's more, Gunther knew his fingerprints would be in her living room. Whether or not that was enough evidence to convict him, he wasn't sure. After all, it was circumstantial. But it didn't look good.

Gunther had to make a quick decision. He could acknowledge his visit with Velma the previous evening, or he could keep silent and wait to see how things developed. He decided to wait. It was necessary to focus his full attention on Inspector Watts who was in the process of speaking.

"The crime that was committed last Monday was far more complicated than would appear at first glance." Watts paused to let this information sink in. "The victim had several enemies, any one of whom could have killed him.

"When my partner and I started investigating this murder, we were working on the assumption that only one killer was involved because only one wound killed him. The second, smaller wound, at the victim's temple, confounded us. If it was the killer's intention to dispatch of Mr. D'Agosta by striking him on the back of the skull, then why the need to deliver a much lighter blow at the temple?

"We discussed this from several angles. First, we thought the lighter blow on the side of the head might have been made to render the victim vulnerable. The boy was a healthy seventeen-year-old who was strong and physically fit. He certainly could have defended himself if he had seen the attack coming. But he didn't. He was taken by surprise—with *both* blows.

"From the pathologist's report, we know the lethal blow was the one to the back of the head—a blow that was delivered with substantial force. The second blow, the non-lethal one to the temple, was delivered with much less force, leading us to believe that the individual who delivered this blow had the rage to react with violence but not the physical strength to create significant damage.

"This led us to the conclusion that the blows were delivered by two different people and that the blows came from two different weapons.

"If we operate under the assumption that these two people were not accomplices, but rather were acting independently, then we have to look at the possibility of two different motivations.

"In the case of the smaller, less lethal wound, we might assume it was the result of a woman's attempt at self-defense. This would make sense for several reasons. First of all, the nature of the deceased was such that he was more than simply a promiscuous adolescent. He was, in fact, a potentially dangerous predator. And from the evidence received through testimony at this school, he was unlikely to take "no" for an answer. It would be easy to see how a woman who found herself backed into a corner would grab at anything she could use in order to protect herself.

"And we believe that is exactly what happened." Watts focused on one particular teacher. "Isn't that so, Miss Gauvin?"

Julie's shoulders began to shake almost uncontrollably. Magda put an arm around her to steady her.

"Yes!" she cried, dabbing at her eyes with a crumpled tissue. "Dino showed up in my classroom about fifteen minutes after I opened up," she began. "He said he needed to get ready for a test later that afternoon, so I allowed him to stay. I honestly thought it would be all right. He had never said or done anything improper to me. I really thought he was harmless."

She began to sniffle and Magda handed her another tissue. She blew her nose.

"It was a few minutes later that he walked to the portable door and locked it. I was confused, but not alarmed. But then he started moving rapidly towards me, and he had this weird look on his face. Before I knew it, he had grabbed me by the shoulders and spun me around. When I expressed outrage, he called me a cocktease. That was when I knew I was in real trouble.

"Just as he was about to kiss me on the mouth, I spied a snow globe on the corner of my desk and lunged for it. Then I smashed it against the side of the head as hard as I could. He staggered backwards, called me a bitch and stumbled out of the door."

"Why didn't you tell anyone about this before now?" Mike asked gently.

"There just wasn't time. Period One was about to start, and then later, when we heard the news about the murder, I was afraid I might have actually killed him. I just panicked. I didn't know what to do, so I did nothing," she began to sob. "I'm sorry. I'm so, so sorry."

"So, you didn't see him after he left your room?"

"No. After waiting a few minutes to make sure he wasn't going to come back, I ran to the washroom in the main building and splashed water on my face. Then I raced back so as not to be late when students started showing up at 7:45. Believe me, all I could think of was to get back to my classroom as quickly as possible."

All eyes were fastened on Julie who sat pale-faced, wringing her hands in her lap. Watts cleared his throat.

"So, let me see if I have this correct, Miss Gauvin," he began calmly. "The deceased attempted to assault you, and you hit him in the temple with the snow globe in order to defend yourself. Then, according to your own words, he staggered out the door, and you never saw him again. Is that correct?"

"Yes." Julie's voice held the vaguest hint of uncertainty. It might have been the result of nervousness or it might have been that she was leaving something out of her story. The inspector wasn't sure which.

He turned his attention to the rest of the staff.

"If, as Miss Gauvin alleges, the victim was staggering when he left her classroom, then it is safe to assume this was the result of being dazed by the blow to the temple. This rendered him unable to recognize danger and respond appropriately when caught off guard by someone who approached him from behind.

"This fact is supported by the pathologist's findings. Mr. D'Agosta was struck with a blunt object by someone who stood over him as the boy was on his knees in the field next to the parking lot. In such a position, the victim presented the killer with the perfect opportunity to strike."

Several teachers squirmed in their seats. According to the scenario that the inspector had just painted, it was possible that any one of them could have been the killer.

Watts took notice of the growing tension in the room. It was time to turn up the heat.

"Now let us look at some of the forensic evidence," he said, guiding the discourse in a different direction. "Microscopic particles of rosewood—the very kind of wood found in the mallets used in this school's shop room—were taken from the victim's skull."

Gunther bolted out of his chair. "You can't pin this on me! Wood carving kits exists in every school shop in the city, and what's more, they're all made out of rosewood!"

"Assuming what you say is true, Mr. Grossman, we still have to ferret out all the facts of the case before coming to any conclusion."

He turned to the middle-aged woman who had been listening carefully to his every word. "Miss Malinsky, your walking stick is made of rosewood and is also capable of being a weapon. Is that not true, Miss Malinsky?"

Magda sat up straight. "Of course. My walking stick is as sturdy as any club. I already described it to you in a previous conversation." She sat back primly in her chair.

Watts studied her briefly.

"Yes, I remember the story of your walking stick," he said. "I also remember that you said you threatened young Mr. D'Agosta."

Magda squared her shoulders. "I never said I threatened him, Inspector," she said with great distinction. "I said that I showed him a move in martial arts that would kill him in seconds. It was a selective suggestion, not a threat. There's a difference."

"And did he take you seriously, Miss Malinsky?"

"What do you think?"

Watts was about to say 'I think he would have been a fool not to,' when Paul approached him and whispered in his ear.

"My assistant has suggested that we have a bathroom break. If you need to leave for the washroom," he announced, "you will be accompanied by a uniformed officer who will stand guard outside the washroom door. We will reconvene in approximately fifteen minutes."

Elaine and Julie both headed for the door; Armand stood up and stretched; Magda stared off into space. And Gunther remained where he was, sitting glumly in his chair.

Nerves were starting to fray.

CHAPTER 35
GIRL TALK

4:45 p.m.

Elaine leaned across the porcelain sink and peered intently at her reflection in the washroom mirror. Retrieving a cosmetic wand from her purse, she used it to touch up her unruly eyebrows while Julie stood silently by, kneading the knots in the back of her neck.

"You killed him, didn't you?" Elaine said suddenly, not taking her eyes away from the mirror.

Julie spun around to stare at the woman making the astonishing accusation. She was about to say something nasty in return, but then a thought struck her. Elaine's outrageous comment was so completely out of character, so utterly uncalled for, there had to be a reasonable explanation. Julie decided to bide her time before responding.

She splashed cold water on her eyes and cheeks, pulled a paper towel from the dispenser and began patting her face, drop by drop until she felt she had regained her composure.

"Why would you say a thing like that, Elaine," she said coolly.

"As the inspector pointed out, facts are facts," the older woman said bluntly. "You and Dino were alone together in your room while it was still dark outside. He used the opportunity to try to attack you, and there was no one to stop him. What choice did you have?" Keeping her eyes glued to her reflection in the mirror, Elaine fished a tube of lipstick out her purse and applied it with great aplomb to her generous mouth.

Julie was having trouble holding onto her temper. What the hell was wrong with this woman? Normally Elaine was just a sweet, agreeable old tabby who swapped stories with her in the faculty lounge over a cup of herbal tea. The young teacher had always found her older coworker's company enjoyable, unlike other staff members who always had something to complain about—the mouthy kids, the heavy workload, the hostile public. The list was endless.

But Elaine was never one of those teachers. She always stressed how appreciative she was of the fact that she was still part of a profession she loved. It colored her every conversation. No, Elaine was usually sunny and upbeat. So this sudden turn in behavior was truly startling. And for the woman to actually accuse her of killing one of her students was simply incomprehensible.

Elaine carefully recapped her lipstick and put it back in her purse. "Look at this way, Julie, dear. You had the means. You had the motive. You had the time. And, as far as I'm concerned, you're the perfect candidate to have killed the poor boy." She smoothed her hair down with the palms of her hands and glanced at the effect in the mirror with some misgivings.

"Not that I owe you any explanation," Julie said tightly, "but didn't you hear the inspector say that the wound inflicted by the snow globe wasn't fatal—that the blow that killed Dino came from a different weapon—something made out of rosewood? Those are the facts, lady! And isn't the school of mathematics based on facts—not speculation. Or is the new math taught these days nothing but guesswork and fanciful thinking?"

"I'm only going by appearances," Elaine sniffed. "Dino was good looking and charming. Maybe *you* were the one who led him on? Maybe he approached you because he knew he could? And maybe you panicked after you realized that you had gone too far? It is possible, isn't it? After all, Dino was hard to resist."

"Hard to resist?!" Now Julie turned on the older woman. "Are you sure you're talking about me—and not *you*?"

"Me! I could have been his grandmother! Get serious." Elaine quickly closed her purse and started for the door.

"Old enough to be his grandmother?" Julie snorted. "As if that made any difference to Dino. The boy was calculating. And he knew his power over women. Is it possible that you had something he wanted?" she sneered. "So, what could it have been, I wonder? And what did he use to get it?"

"My, my. Look at the time. We better be getting back." Elaine said, placing her hand on the doorknob.

"That's it, isn't it?" Julie said. "He was blackmailing you! That's the reason you want to point the finger at me. It's a case of misdirection, isn't it, *Mrs.* Richardson? Shift the focus away from you—away from something you want desperately to hide?"

Elaine looked around nervously in case anyone was in the stalls. "C'mon," she urged. "The inspector will be waiting for us."

Julie wasn't budging.

"What did he have on you?" she demanded. "Did you sleep with him? Is that it?"

Elaine was stung by the young teacher's remark. "I'm not a slut, Julie," she said indignantly. "I don't sleep with my students."

"And yet you implied that I did."

Elaine closed her eyes and inhaled deeply. She seemed to be coming out of a trance. "I'm sorry, Julie. It's just that... I'm worried." She paused. "This case has me unhinged. I don't know what I'm saying half the time. I'm sorry."

Julie gave the matter a moment's thought. Elaine *sounded* sincere, but one could never tell with absolute certainty if people really meant what they were saying. Sometimes you had give people the benefit of the doubt. Julie decided that was what she would do in this instance.

"I know, I know," the young teacher sighed. "We're all under a terrible strain. No one seems to be themselves anymore. I guess, under the circumstances, it's natural to imagine all sorts of crazy things. Frankly, the person I wonder about is Velma. I think if anyone were having an affair with that teenage Casanova, it would have been her. But, since she's not here to defend herself, and apparently, somebody was after her too, we'll have to put those thoughts aside."

Just then an officer knocked on the door. "It's time to go, ladies. Let's get moving."

Dutifully Julie and Elaine fell in line and filed out of the washroom, quietly closing the door behind them.

CHAPTER 36
HOUR OF RECKONING, PART II

5:00 p.m.

"All right people, I don't need to remind you why we're all here." The inspector spoke sternly as everyone quickly resumed their seats.

"Yesterday," he said, "I mentioned that I paid a visit to the board office where I requisitioned the employment records of everyone working at Fairmont—"

"Okay! Okay!" Gunther jumped to his feet, sweat glistening on his wide forehead. "I was young for god's sake! It was my first year teaching. I made a mistake. So sue me!"

He sat back down dejectedly.

Magda guffawed. "So, Macho Man, what was this mistake that you made?"

"I accidentally walked through the wrong door. Is that a crime? It was a large school, and I got lost on the way to the boys' locker room. How was I to know that the girls' dressing room was located in the same corridor?" He ran the back of his hand across his damp forehead. "Jeez! I never heard so much screaming in my life!"

"And you got in trouble for this *how*?" The inspector seemed intrigued, but not surprised.

"Well, that damn uptight girls' Phys Ed teacher reported me to the principal. She accused me of voyeurism and suggested I should be disciplined."

The room was silent – a silence that Gunther found unsettling.

"Look, what happened was an accident for god's sake!" he blurted out while shifting uncomfortably in his chair.

"Let me get this straight," Watts said. "You were going to the *boys'* locker room?"

"Yeah. What's so unusual about that?"

"Nothing—if you're a boys' PE teacher."

"I was the football coach, for crying out loud! Where else would I be going?"

"I see." Watts noted Gunther's discomfort, as did the rest of the people in the staffroom.

"So you're the one with a questionable reputation at the board office!" Armand exclaimed with glee. "And Velma had to have known. How did you manage to keep her quiet?" he snickered.

"Wait a minute." Julie spoke up. "We don't know for sure that Gunther, or anyone else, got in trouble at the board office. The Inspector never told us what he found out there, so we're not in a position to jump to conclusions."

The inspector nodded. "Miss Gauvin is right. All I said was that I discovered information that was critical to the case."

"What the *hell* does that mean?" demanded Armand who had run out of patience.

"That is classified police business," Watts responded.

Magda was becoming irritated herself. "Then why bring it up in the first place?"

—

Why indeed?

Staff Inspector Watts had no intention of naming names. As he explained to his partner when they had met in the school parking lot just prior to the meeting the previous day, he only intended to use the information discovered at the board office to flush people out of hiding.

Paul had been disturbed by what he was hearing. To learn that the person guilty of sexual misconduct with an underage boy at another school was none other than Fairmont's VP had shocked the young rookie. On the other hand, knowing Velma's history with Dino, it certainly made sense. What *didn't* make sense was the fact that Velma Vorchek wasn't just transferred to another school, she was actually *promoted* to the position of vice principal!

Thinking about the unfairness of it all, Paul was reminded of the words he had once expressed to Mike: *It's a sick world.*

—

"Listen," Magda said firmly, "I've been at this school my entire career with never a hint of scandal, Inspector. So whatever information you found at the board office can't be about me." She turned to the math teacher. "What about you, Elaine? Any deep dark secrets in your past? Speak up. We're all dying to know," she said teasingly, but Elaine took Magda's remark seriously. Too seriously, in fact.

"Oh, God," the older teacher groaned. "I was just trying to help the boy."

Magda's eyes grew wide with astonishment. Not for a minute did she suspect Elaine of any impropriety, but the science teacher's comments had triggered an unexpected confession. "What boy?" she blurted out.

"Dino," Elaine cried out. "Dino D'Agosta!"

Julie was just about to say something when the inspector held up his hand to stop her.

"I know it was foolish," Elaine admitted, her lips trembling, "but I did it in all innocence. I really didn't know what the boy was like." The woman sat miserably twisting her hands in her lap.

Julie raised the question that was on everyone's mind. "What did you do that was so foolish?"

"I invited him to my house for a tutoring session." She bowed her head. "I don't know how it happened, but I woke up in my bed with the boy staring at me from across the room."

"What?!" Magda stared at her in disbelief. "Are you saying you slept with him?"

"No. No. At least, if I did, I have no memory of it." When she felt she had regained control of herself, she began to speak. "I showed him a coaster, that my late husband had made for me and it triggered so many memories, I got caught up in emotion. Also, I had offered him some hot chocolate for our tutoring session, and I had laced mine with Bailey's." She stopped to wipe her eyes with a damp tissue.

"Anyway, the alcohol must have gone to my head, and I ended up passed out and on my bed. When I woke up, the boy was sitting in a chair on the other side of the room watching me. He said nothing happened, and I believed him." She shook her head sadly. "I knew then I had made a major mistake. I insisted that he leave immediately and I followed him to the front door to make sure that he did."

"Okay, so you were unwise—definitely naïve," Magda started to say.

"Don't forget stupid," interjected Armand. He turned to the distraught woman. "You really don't have any sense for someone your age, do you, Elaine?"

"Oh, come on," Julie chided. "Dino was a con artist—one of the best. He fooled me. I thought he was harmless, and look at the trouble I got into. Give the woman a break!"

"It gets worse." Elaine hesitated before continuing. "Later that same evening, he telephoned. He said he had my special wooden coaster and that he wouldn't tell Velma about the incident at my house if I gave him an 'A' on the mid-term exam. But he lied. He did tell Velma because I saw my coaster in the principal's office when I was in there being interviewed by the inspector."

"One has to wonder just exactly how much that wretched woman *did* know," Magda chimed in, "and who her source was."

"Don't you mean *does* know?" Gunther said. "She's not dead. And isn't it obvious. Her source was Dino. I doubt there was anyone at school who had more dirt on the staff than that boy did."

"Well, I wonder," Armand said, thinking out loud, "what dirt could he have had on Velma?"

Elaine snorted. "If she had my coaster stashed on Dino's behalf in the principal's private office, my guess is that the woman knew the boy intimately. He certainly implied as much the night he called to blackmail me."

"An intimate relationship?!" Magda sounded incredulous. "Between a woman in her sixties and a boy of seventeen?"

"Jealous?" Armand snickered.

"I'm not the one who would have been jealous," Magda quipped.

"All right, people, it's getting late," Watts said. "We have a few more things to discuss before we wrap up this meeting."

The inspector's announcement had hearts sinking. Everyone was more than eager to go home—that is, *almost* everyone.

CHAPTER 37
"ARREST THE BASTARD!"

6:10p.m.

Armand leaned back in his chair and grinned wickedly. "Well, what do you know? Velma has the hots for Dino and carries on an affair right under our noses. Sweet! And our mild-mannered math teacher wakes up in her bed with Dino watching her from across the room while our innocent little English teacher foils an attempted rape with a whack from a snow globe." Armand chuckled. "And I thought this meeting was going to be boring."

"Well, what else matters but your entertainment?" Gunther shot back. "Isn't that right, *Tinker Bell*?"

Armand focused a laser look of hatred at the shop teacher. "And who were you fucking while all this was going on? Was it our long-legged VP—the one you're constantly trying to sell as 'not that bad'?"

"For God's sake, Armand, keep a civil tongue in your head." Julie exclaimed. She was puzzled by way the inspector wasn't saying anything. So was everyone else.

Armand ignored her, turning his attention instead to Watts.

"Well, what about it, Inspector? Weren't you the one to reveal that the murder weapon was made out of rosewood—the exact kind of wood that the mallets in the school's shop are made of? Is that why your forensics people returned to the school this morning and ended up coming out of Gunther's classroom carrying God knows what?" His eyes danced merrily. "You know, rumor has it that Gunther and the dearly departed had a thing going—that is, until Dino got bored and dumped the guy." Armand placed his hand on his heart and sighed. "Ahhh... unrequited love. Is there anything sadder?"

Gunther glared fiercely at the French teacher. He was about to utter a stinging retort when Magda jumped in. She stared hard at him. "You were having an affair with a student? Isn't that something that could have gotten you fired?"

Gunther turned sideways so he could face her head-on. "Not that it's any of your business, Miss Malinsky, but we were *not* having an affair. I felt sorry for the kid after he told me about his mother—the woman's a monster. I had a rough childhood myself, so I thought I'd help brighten the kid up by taking him to a hockey game one Saturday. When I came back from the restroom, I saw Dino was gone, and as it turned out, so was the cash in my wallet that I had left in my jacket on my seat.

Student Body

"The next time I saw the boy, I accused him of stealing. He denied it, but from then on he started showing up late to class and then skipping whenever he felt like it. I called him out on his attendance and attitude, and he got nasty. So, in the end, I kicked him out of the course."

"*That's* why you kicked him out—a beautiful boy who played you for a fool?" Armand scoffed. "*He was skipping class?!*"

"Oh, for Pete's sake, Armand!" Elaine jumped in before Gunther had a chance to speak. "The kid played everyone for a fool. If you had something he wanted, he managed to get his hooks into you. I should know," she said bitterly.

"Elaine's little outburst aside," Armand sniffed, "are you trying to tell the rest of us that you weren't in love with Dino, Mr. Macho Man?"

Gunther looked disgusted. "No, I wasn't in love with Dino. All I did was try to inject some normalcy into the boy's life by taking him to a hockey game. I had no ulterior motive."

Armand pouted. "Put any kind of spin you want on it, but it's clear to folks around here that you had the hots for the boy or he wouldn't have found you such an easy mark."

Gunther was about to sputter out an answer when Julie turned on him in outrage. "What does that say about me, Armand? Did Dino decide to attack me because he imagined I secretly wanted him? Is that what you're saying?"

"We're getting away from the issue here," Armand huffed indignantly. "We were talking about the forensics people going into Gunther's shop this morning." He turned to Inspector Watts. "Did they find what they were looking for? I mean, why go to all the trouble of returning to the scene of the crime if they didn't know what they were looking for." Armand leaned back in his chair and folded his arms across his chest. "Well?" he smiled smugly.

Watts decided to humor him. "Yes. They knew what they were looking for. And you're right, it was a mallet—one with blood on it."

"And did they find it?"

Everyone leaned forward to hear the inspector's answer.

"Yes," he said quietly.

"That's it then!" Armand cried excitedly. "It had to be Gunther. He had motive, he had access, and he had opportunity. Everyone knows he arrives early. So one morning he spies Dino coming out of Julie's portable. But the kid isn't walking in a straight line. So Gunther stands back and watches the kid stagger into the field beside the parking lot. That's his chance. He sneaks up behind the boy and bashes him on the back of the head."

Armand jumped to his feet. "What are you waiting for?" he screamed hysterically. "Arrest the bastard!"

Gunther's face turned purple with rage. "You crazy, nasty, malicious little prick?!"

"People! People! Watch your language!" Magda scolded. "The killer could have been any one of us. Several teachers

Student Body

here worked in the portables, and we all had access to the empty field beside the parking lot. And, not to put too fine a point on it, we all hated Dino!"

Watts decided it was time to step in.

"Miss Malinsky is right. Any one of you could have been the killer. The murder of Dino D'Agosta was a crime of passion. Hatred was the motive, but not hatred for the victim. In this case, the hatred was for the killer's rival."

Gunther was stupefied. "What are you saying!?"

"What I'm saying, plain and simple," Inspector Watts said, "is that the killer had not one, but two intended victims—the boy he loved and the man he hated."

"But, Inspector," Magda said, "there was only one body."

"That's right, Miss Malinsky, but there were two intended victims. One to be murdered and one to take the fall."

"Take the fall?" She looked perplexed. "What are you talking about?"

"It's simple," Watts said. "One of you was set up."

"Set up?" Gunther rubbed his forehead. "By whom?"

"As a matter of fact," said Mike, turning his attention directly to the shop teacher, "your competition."

"My competition?" he asked dully.

"Yes. The man who was convinced you were having an affair with the boy he idolized." He took a step forward.

"Gunther Grossman, meet your completion, Mr. Armand Saint-Yves."

CHAPTER 38
THE COMPETITION

6:30 p.m.

"That's absurd!" Armand protested hotly. "I don't even own a mallet, for god's sake. And I already told you, it was so cold and blustery that day. I was in no mood to linger in the parking lot, much less the vacant field beside it."

"So you got out of your car and immediately proceeded to the main building? Is that what you're saying?" Watts said.

"Yes."

"That's not what you said in our interview," Watts reminded him. "You said that you went to your portable as soon as you arrived at school. Then you wrote instructions on the board to keep the class busy while you were gone to the office. Are you changing your story?"

"No. No," he stammered. "I remember now. I went to my classroom first, and *then* I went to the main building." He smoothed his hair back awkwardly with the palm of his hand. "I must be getting old. My memory sometimes slips."

The inspector moved until he was standing directly in front of Armand.

"Let's imagine a different scenario, shall we? Suppose you didn't go to your classroom as soon as you arrived at school. Suppose you decided to go to the office *before* going to your classroom.

"It's still semi-dark outside, and you don't see anyone around as you're walking through the parking lot. But then you spot a woozy Dino reeling about. The boy is blinded by the heavy snowfall and staggers into the empty field next door. A quick look around assures you there are no witnesses, so you follow him, and when he falls to his knees, you sneak up behind and bludgeon him with the mallet you had purchased weeks earlier in anticipation of just such an opportunity. Everything is in place—the lack of witnesses—the blinding snowstorm—the disabled target—there would never be a better time.

"So you've killed the boy, but now you've got a problem. You're holding a bloodied murder weapon and students and teachers will be arriving any minute. You wrap the mallet in your scarf, stuff it in the oversized briefcase you had bought months ago for the same purpose, and then dash back to your own portable where you can safely hide it until everyone has gone home for the day.

"Before you leave your classroom, you quickly jot down instructions on the blackboard to make it appear you had gone immediately to your classroom. Once that's completed, you are now ready to pretend you are going to the main building for the first time."

"Really!" Armand sneered scornfully. "And how do you suppose I happen to conveniently have a wooden mallet on my person as I'm making my way to the office."

Watts stared confidently at the small man eyeing him warily.

"You yourself admitted to being the person on call the day Gunther went to court to finalize his divorce. Once you had access to the shop portable, it would have been easy for you to notice the wood carving kit. Then you knew exactly how to incriminate Gunther. It was a simple matter of shopping for an identical kit and then keeping one of the mallets in your briefcase to use at a moment's notice. You follow me?"

People hung on the inspector's every word.

"After that," Watts said, "you waited for the right moment to strike. It came the day Julie walloped the boy with her snow globe, thus rendering him incapable of defending himself.

"It was perfect. With one mighty blow you punished the beautiful boy with whom you were obsessed and implicated the man who had belittled and tormented you for years."

Armand said nothing. He seemed to be in a trance, his face flushed with an odd look of rapture.

"To continue," Watts said, ignoring Armand's odd expression, "the next step in your plan was to substitute the bloodied mallet for a clean one in the school's shop.

"When you heard me say at yesterday's meeting that the forensic unit would be returning to Fairmont this morning to inspect *inside* the portables, you knew you had a narrow window of opportunity during which to make the exchange.

"Detective Bunyan and I were already convinced of your guilt, but we needed hard evidence, so we staked out the area all night and waited for you to show up.

"We watched you park your car a few houses down from the school's parking lot. We saw you take an object out of the trunk of your car, and then make your way to the shop portable.

"When you exited the classroom, Detective Bunyan took your picture with his infrared camera. He took another picture when you returned to your car—this time of your license plate. Now we had evidence that would stand up in court.

"Moreover, during my interview with Mr. Grossman earlier in the week, he revealed some pertinent information. On the bottom of each mallet belonging to the school are etched the tiny initials FH for Fairmont High. When forensics examines the mallet with Dino's blood on it later today, they're not going to find those initials on it. Are they, Mr. Saint-Yves?"

Student Body

—

The French teacher closed his eyes and retreated deeply into a world of his own. He smiled softly to himself as he savored the memory of the morning of the murder.

It had been exceptionally cold that day, and a snowstorm seemed to appear from out of nowhere. As he hastened across the parking lot towards the main building, he spotted Dino stumbling around in the semi-darkness—drunk or possibly stoned—it didn't matter. The boy had fallen to his knees and was quite helpless.

There was no time to lose. Quickly he retrieved the wood carving mallet from his briefcase and quietly snuck up behind the defenseless boy. Then he raised his arm and brought the mallet crashing down on the back of his skull.

What a feeling! It was exhilarating.

But soon cars would be arriving. He had to act fast. He rushed back to his portable, locked the murder weapon inside his private cupboard, then jotted down a few words of instructions for his students on the blackboard. After that, he walked in an unhurried manner to the main building to collect his mail—just as he would have done on any other school day.

It was all so easy.

After the last class, he would simply put the mallet in his briefcase, walk leisurely to his car and no one would be the wiser. That evening he would dispose of his briefcase—a big, ugly thing which he hated but which had been necessary to his carefully thought out plans. After that, it was a simple matter of making a quick trip to the mall to purchase a replacement.

He had been clever—oh, so very clever. And it had been fun—fooling the police, fooling his colleagues. They weren't nearly as smart as they thought they were. No. He was the smart one.

But he was tired now. He stood up and stretched as if waking up from a deeply satisfying sleep. The show was over, and it was time to go home.

But then he remembered, he *couldn't* go home. He was stuck in the staffroom, surrounded by people who were not his friends. *Not his friends*. He had to get out of there.

He took one step forward and stopped. It was the sight of the uniformed guard at the door, his hand resting lightly on his revolver that gave Armand pause. Reluctantly he slumped back down in his chair, his shoulders drooping like a wilted flower.

Now he knew there would be no escape. All his careful calculations, all his meticulous planning—all for nothing. Dino, the love of his life was dead, and Gunther, his mortal enemy, was going free. It was over.

Or was it?

Maybe, with a little luck there was another way he could still win. That is if he played his cards right.

Student Body

Gunther glared at him fiercely.

"You vile, despicable thing—you. Killing the boy and trying to pin the wrap on me! God! If only Velma were here to listen to this…" A stricken look swept across his face. "Velma! Poor Velma!" he said, shaking his head in disbelief, "that she should end up hospitalized and in a coma…"

Gunther's words suddenly reminded everyone of Velma, who, in the excitement, had been all but forgotten.

Lost in thought, no one spoke until the silence was broken by Magda. "Yes," she said thoughtfully. "What *did* happen to Velma?"

CHAPTER 39
COLLATERAL DAMAGE

6:45 p.m.

"Yes," Julie echoed, "what *did* happen to Velma? How does she tie in with Dino's murder?"

"I believe Mr. Grossman is the person who can supply some answers to that mystery," Watts said evenly.

All eyes turned towards the shop teacher who was running his hand through his hair as if to keep his head from exploding. At first Gunther had felt nothing but rage at being set up by Armand to take the wrap for Dino's murder, but that was soon followed by a surge of relief after listening to the inspector recite evidence that effectively cleared him. Maybe it was time to make a clean breast of it.

"You knew all along, didn't you, Inspector?"

"I suspected as much, but I didn't know for sure."

"Okay. Here it is: I was at Velma's house last night, but she was all right when I left."

"So you feigned ignorance and told no one the truth." Watts said. "What made you think *that* was the best course of action?"

"I panicked. I figured my fingerprints would be all over her place. Any way you look at, I would be a prime suspect."

"Withholding information from the police is a serious matter. You could be facing a charge of obstruction of justice," Watts commented wryly.

"Me?! I'm not the one who killed the boy. Why aren't you arresting that son of a bitch, Armand?"

Actually everyone else was wondering the same thing. What was the inspector waiting for? Was he looking to find out what connection, if any, existed between Armand, Velma, and Gunther? Was the cagey old cop hoping to set another trap?

Finally Gunther could stand it no longer. "I didn't attack her, for god's sake!" he blurted out. "I swear it!"

Watts ignored his outburst. "What time did you arrive at her townhouse?" he asked casually.

"I don't know. About 8:30 I think."

"And when did you leave?"

"I can't remember. Maybe 9:10 or 9:15."

"You were there for 45 minutes? Why did you leave so early?"

"Velma got sick. I had brought a bottle of wine and we ordered Chinese food, but then she said she wasn't feeling well and ran off to the bathroom."

"You were in her house for approximately 45 minutes while you ordered food, and then she got sick, so you left? Is that correct?"

"Yeah."

"What did you talk about?"

"The staff meeting mostly. I was curious about your remarks about visiting the board office and discovering *information* critical to the case. I asked her if she knew what you were referring to and she denied it. Then I implied that I already knew because Dino had told me. That was a lie. He hadn't told me a thing. But I'd bet the farm that Velma told him."

"Really?" said Watts. "A vice principal would tell a student such confidential information?"

"She had a real thing for Dino. What can I say?"

Magda looked disgusted. "How did that woman get away with it?"

Gunther shrugged "Well, my guess is there were certain members of the board who had a 'thing' for Velma as well."

Watts was anxious to return to his line of questioning. "During the time that you were at her house, did you quarrel?"

"No. That wasn't the name of the game."

"Oh?" The inspector was intrigued. "What *was* the name of the game?"

Gunther grinned boyishly. "Seduction."

Magda rolled her eyes. "And yet she got sick."

"You implied that Dino had been given key information by Velma and that he then gave that information to you," Watts said, ignoring Magda's sarcastic comment. "Why would Dino tell you such a powerful secret?"

Gunther sighed. "I already *told* you, Dino didn't tell me a thing. I was merely teasing Velma. Call me a cad, but I was curious. That's all."

"So, to review the facts," Watts said, "you spent time with both Dino and Velma. Were you jealous of Dino's relationship with Velma?"

"Of course not! I wasn't in love with either one of them. As I already said, I tried to befriend the boy because he had a rotten home life and there was no father figure in his life. It was different with Velma. We were lovers occasionally. Anyway, I didn't hurt Dino, and I didn't hurt Velma."

"Did you bring her an American Beauty rose or have one sent to her house?"

Gunther frowned. "No. Why do you ask?"

"Because somebody did. And that somebody bashed her on the back of the head when she bent down to pick it up at her front door."

Gunther blanched. "I assure you she was fine when I left."

"Can you prove it?"

Armand sat up straight, all his senses heightened. His plan might work after all.

"No, I can't," he said reluctantly. "I only found out about what happened earlier today."

"You're a liar!" Armand screamed. "You lured her outside and then you tried to kill her!"

"That's absurd! If I wanted to kill her, why wouldn't I do it inside the privacy of her home, away from any witnesses who might be out on the street?"

"All right, all right, settle down." Watts turned towards the other suspects and began to speak in a calm, controlled voice. "Gunther didn't lure Velma out her front door. Someone else did. And for a very good reason."

"He hated Velma?" Julie ventured a guess.

"No. Velma was collateral damage. She had something the killer needed in order to carry out his plan to frame Gunther."

Magda, who had been listening carefully to the discussions going on around her, had been trying to fit the pieces of Watts's scenario together into a single whole, but there had been a piece missing. With the inspector's last statement, the puzzle was now complete.

"Of course!" she exclaimed. "The killer needed access to the shop portable so he could exchange the murder weapon for one of the clean mallets stored there."

"That's right," Watts said. "All the teachers had keys to their own classrooms but not to the other classrooms.

"Except Velma!" Julie exclaimed. "Only she and the caretakers would have had a master key to all the classrooms!"

Watts nodded. "Knowing this, the killer followed Velma home and hid out of sight among the tall cedars clustered at the end of her unit. There he had a perfect vantage point to observe anyone coming and going without being seen. It was a simple matter of waiting, bait in hand, for the right time to put his plan in motion.

"Then fortune seemed to smile on him. Who should show up to pay her a visit? None other than Gunther carrying a bottle of wine. This was perfect! Here was another crime he could pin on his adversary. So he remained hidden in the shadows until he saw Gunther leave."

"Then he came out of hiding and planted the vase with the American Beauty rose in it on her front porch," Elaine said excitedly, "that way she would have to bend down to pick it up."

"Exactly," Watts said. "He knocked her out so he would have access to her house. It was a coldly calculated move, and he didn't really care whether or not the blow was fatal. His agenda was to find the master key. Velma was merely collateral damage."

Julie looked at the French teacher in horror.

"So you clubbed her just like you did Dino. What kind of a monster are you?!"

"Me!" he screamed in outrage. "*Me*! A monster? They're the monsters! That selfish *fuck* Dino and that ball busting bitch Velma. And Gunther! The scum of the earth! I should have killed him long ago. Instead, I had to content myself with seeing him sent to the slammer for the rest of his life. Yes, that would have been fun," he said ruefully. "Unfortunately, thanks to the interference of the good inspector here, that's not going to happen."

Suddenly Armand bolted upright, knocking over Elaine's chair and sending her sprawling to the floor. Watts moved quickly to offer her his hand and gently pulled her back up just as a glint of steel flashed past his eyes, and Julie screamed. Armand was clutching a razor-sharp pocket knife and waving it wildly at Gunther's head.

It was then that Bunyan sprang into action. He grasped Armand from behind and kneed him in the back of his legs, throwing the small man off balance and forcing him to drop the knife. While Armand thrashed about helplessly, Bunyan pinned his arms behind his back and cuffed him. He then read him his rights and hustled the French teacher to the door where the armed guard was waiting to take him to police headquarters.

Just before he stepped through the doorway, Armand turned to face his accusers. Time for one last curtain call …

"They deserved it," he shouted, proudly thrusting out his chest. "Every one of them! First there was that little tin-god, Dino, enticing me to fall in love with him. It was fun for him to watch me make a fool of myself. And Velma, that man-hating bitch, using every opportunity to push me around because she got off on power. Yes, they deserved it, both of them. And as for Gunther, that prick, if I had had more time, I would have— "

He was cut short by the officer shoving him through the door.

Julie and Magda stared open mouthed at Armand's retreating back. His surprisingly spiteful tirade had left them speechless.

Elaine also was momentarily stunned. She turned wide-eyed to Watts who had been standing nearby, quietly observing the scene with profound interest.

"Inspector," she tugged at his sleeve.

It was obvious something was on her mind, so he bent down to where he could hear her better. "Yes," he answered.

"I wanted to thank you for helping me up from the floor," she whispered. Then her eye caught sight of something that made her scream.

Bev Bachmann

Blood was pouring out of a deep gash on Gunther's neck.

CHAPTER 40
"A BEAKER FULL OF ACID"

9:30 p.m.

Julie's young face was lined with worry. She, Magda and Elaine had been sitting in emergency for what seemed like hours when an intern in green scrubs carrying a clipboard happened to be passing by. Julie immediately jumped in front of him, blocking his way.

"Is he going to live?" she demanded.

The busy doctor, momentarily taken aback, stopped in his tracks. He stared down at an obviously frazzled but very attractive young woman.

"Is *who* going to live?" he asked agreeably.

"Gunther Grossman. The man who was brought here from Fairmont High about two hours ago."

"Grossman? Let's have a look." He flipped through the charts on his clipboard. "There's a Grossman in exam room number 8. It says here the patient sustained a puncture wound to the neck three millimeters from the carotid artery." He stopped to study the anxious young woman standing before him. "Is he a friend of yours? Perhaps a family member?"

"Neither. He's a shop teacher." She knew the moment she said it, she sounded like an idiot, but she was too emotionally exhausted to care.

"He's a teacher?"

The doctor's voice registered surprise. "How did that happen? Breaking up a fight in the halls?" He seemed genuinely interested.

"No. He was stabbed by another teacher," she answered abruptly. The expression on the physician's face made her add quickly, "It's a long story. We have to go."

She grabbed her two colleagues and the three of them started moving quickly down the hall, glancing at the numbers on the examination rooms along the way.

In spite of having to navigate with her walking stick, Magda was the first to arrive at Gunther's room where she called out his name before peeking around the curtain. He was sitting up on a narrow bed dressed in a thin blue hospital gown, a thick wad of dressing taped securely to his neck.

"Hey, Buddy, how you doing?" she greeted him cheerfully while Elaine and Julie looked on with obvious concern.

"I'm okay. I got something for the pain and then some blond cutie came in to check up on me—almost made it worthwhile to be stabbed," he said, shifting his weight on the narrow cot. "Anyway, I'm waiting for a prescription for antibiotics and a tetanus shot." He lowered his voice conspiratorially. "You know they give that shot in the ass—I requested it," he said conspiratorially, "so you ladies might want to stick around for the show," he grinned mischievously.

Julie started to laugh. Magda frowned. Obviously the girl was close to losing it.

"Thanks all the same, Gunther," Magda said. "I think we better get Julie out of here before someone gives her a shot in the ass."

Gunther grinned. "I guess I'm not the only one feeling no pain," he said, tugging at his blanket which had gotten bunched up under his legs. "Say, isn't this the hospital where they took Velma? Does anyone know where she is or what her condition is?"

"I'll see if I can find out," Elaine offered, stepping out into the hallway and disappearing down the long hospital corridor.

Magda reached out and gently patted Gunther's hand.

"It looks like you're going to be laid up for a day or two." She paused to shake her head at him as if she were about to reprimand a naughty school boy. "You know, Gunther, taking Dino to a hockey game could look very suspicious. It might even have jeopardized your job—if people got the wrong idea," she said sternly.

Gunther cast his eyes down. "I know. It was stupid. The boy just seemed so rootless. I couldn't help feeling sorry for him. I had a rough youth myself, so I guess I identified with him. Anyway, let's forget about him and talk about something cheerful, like my plans for the future," he said, sitting up straighter. "I'm almost 53 and I've got a nice little nest egg saved up, so I was toying with the idea of taking early retirement and following a dream I've had for years—opening up my own handmade furniture shop."

"That should keep you out of harm's way," Magda said wryly. "And if you promise to behave yourself and keep your hands off of them, I'll send you ladies from the social club at my church." She smiled sweetly, but she was serious.

"I'm going to need furniture for a bigger apartment when I eventually move," Julie chimed in, "and you'll be the first person I call on."

He raised himself up on his elbows. "I didn't realize you people were my friends." His eyes started to mist, either from gratitude or the effects of the sedative. Either way, the women recognized it was time to leave and quietly slipped out from behind the curtain.

When they spotted Elaine coming down the hall towards them, they rushed toward her. "Well, what's the word on Velma?" Magda asked eagerly.

"She's still in ICU but holding her own. It looks like she will be out of commission for a long time—at least until the end of the school year."

"I'm sure the director and superintendent are already working on the problem," Magda said. "I doubt they're happy with all the notoriety this crime has created. If only we could keep the name of the school out of it."

"I'm afraid it's too late for that," Julie commented. "I saw reporters snooping around the hospital already. There's just no way to keep this thing under wraps, especially when it involves the school's vice principal."

"I know." Magda sighed and shook her head in disbelief. "Hard to imagine that intolerable woman drunk on power and throwing her weight around now confined to a hospital bed, helpless as a baby!"

"Serves her right!" Elaine blurted out bitterly.

Magda said nothing, but Elaine's words put Julie in a thoughtful mood. Did Velma deserve her fate, as Elaine had so passionately declared? Or was there another factor to consider?

It was true that Velma had been heavy-handed in dealing with the staff. From the day she had taken over for Principal Morris, she never let an opportunity go by without reaming someone out about something—no matter how petty or inconsequential. It got so, wherever she went, there was an immediate clearing of the area. But now that the woman was hospitalized and flat on her back, Julie couldn't help but wonder. Did she deserve her fate?

"You know, Elaine," Julie began slowly, sorting through her thoughts as she went along, "you have a right to resent

Velma, but there might be another side to the story. When I was an undergrad, I came across quite a few individuals like her—certifiable control freaks. And after thinking about it, I reached a certain conclusion. Such people are prisoners of their own making. Their world is filled with fear.

"It's as if they go through life carrying a beaker full of acid," she went on, "and every time they meet someone, a little of that acid sloshes over the sides, scalding anyone in their path. But sooner or later, that acid will splash back on them. It's inevitable. No one can carry around that much anger without it searing their soul."

Magda stared at Julie in wonder. "You're quite the philosopher, aren't you, girl? Well, you could be right." She turned to Elaine. "Do you agree with our young friend here, that control freaks create their own misery?" When Elaine didn't answer, Magda prodded her. "Well, what do you think?"

"What do I think?" Elaine was quiet for a moment. "It's possible Julie has a point," she said after giving the matter some thought. "I guess there's some comfort in subscribing to the belief that justice prevails in the end. But if you ask me, there's no way to pretty things up where Velma Vorchek is concerned. That woman is a first-class bitch."

EPILOGUE
TWO WEEKS LATER

10:30 a.m.

Strategically located between Fairmont and a well-known city landmark called The Christie Pitts stood a small Tim Horton's frequented by locals on their way to and from the subway station. It was here on a cold grey Saturday morning a few weeks after the murder of Dino D'Agosta and the assault on Velma Vorchek that Julie was standing in line to place her order.

She scanned the donuts, muffins, and other goodies arrayed on trays displayed behind two large panes of glass. The coffee shop was filling up fast, and a young Vietnamese server with weary eyes was waiting for Julie to make her selection.

"I'll have a raisin tea biscuit and a hot chocolate," she said, digging into her purse for her wallet.

"Toasted with butter?"

Julie looked up. For a split second her mind went back to some of the service type summer jobs she had worked to support herself through university. She understood how difficult it was to cater to the needs of a not always polite public.

"Yes," she said softly, trying to convey a bit of encouragement, if not camaraderie.

Julie grabbed her tray and headed straight for a table by the window where she placed her coat and scarf on the back of her chair before sitting down. Leisurely she stirred her hot chocolate while keeping a look-out for the person who had arranged this meeting. Soon she spotted a tall figure hurrying down the street in the direction of the coffee shop, a plaid grey and green scarf tucked inside his bomber jacket to ward off the chill of a January morning.

Pushing the door open, Detective Paul Bunyan cast a look around the crowd until he spied Julie sitting next to the window, quietly sipping her hot chocolate. He strode briskly over to her table and pulled up a chair.

"Thanks for meeting me on such short notice," he said yanking off his leather gloves and shoving them inside his pockets. He craned his neck around to inspect the growing crowd at the counter. "I guess I should go get in line." For a moment, he seemed reluctant to move, as if he were afraid she would leave as soon as he stepped away from the table.

Julie brought her cup to her lips and blew softly across the foamy surface. "My chocolate is too hot to drink," she said casually. "Why don't you go order yourself something? The service here is usually pretty fast."

"Okay, but this may take a while." He paused tentatively. "Would you like something else while I'm ordering?"

"Sure. Bring me a cup of coffee this time. Small with cream, no sugar." Normally she wouldn't have had so many beverages at one sitting, but Julie understood the principle behind making someone feel comfortable in an awkward situation—give them something to do.

When he returned, he placed a cherry cheese Danish and cup of black coffee on his side of the table and handed over the cup of coffee Julie had requested.

"Thanks." She gave him a smile, carefully removing the lid off her steaming cup. "How are things going at police headquarters? Is Armand going to trial soon?"

Bunyan shook his head; it was obvious that Julie wasn't familiar with the judicial system.

"Well, it depends on how you define *soon*," he said. "It will probably be 18 to 24 months from now. The docket is pretty full." He stopped to take a sip of coffee and a bite out of his Danish. "Of course, this is a high-profile case, so it may be sooner rather than later. The media is eager for details, and they are putting pressure on the department."

"That makes sense," Julie said. "The crimes involves a teacher, a vice-principal, and a student—and not just any student—one who had multiple affairs with both male and female members of the staff. That's bound to stir up public interest, prurient as that interest may be."

"Yeah, well," Paul shrugged. "Sex sells."

Julie nodded in agreement.

Paul decided to change the subject. "Have you heard who the new VP will be? Did Velma get fired, or was she given a leave of absence until she recovers."

"Fired?" Julie stared moodily into her cup of coffee. "It seems we're both naïve about certain realities. The politics of education is just as duplicitous as the workings in the justice system. The truth is that almost no one gets fired from a school. What they usually get is a suspension with pay, and often a transfer—preferably to some unsuspecting school, which isn't given a reason or a choice in the matter."

"You sound cynical."

"That's the way it is. The union protects its members, and the board sweeps everything under the rug." She took a vicious bite out of her tea biscuit. "In any case, when and if she's up for it, Velma is being assigned a new position with the Department of Education as a Curriculum Coordinator." She paused to wipe the back of her mouth with a crumpled napkin.

Paul frowned. "That sounds suspiciously like a promotion."

Julie simply pressed her lips together and nodded.

"So then who's to be the new VP at Fairmont?" he ventured to ask.

"I heard last week that Magda will be taking Velma's place until June. A decision will be made during the summer as to who will continue in the position next fall."

"Magda? Frankly, I think that's a good choice, but what will happen to her classes?"

"They'll be shuffled between the existing science teachers. The department isn't happy about it, but everyone is relieved that Velma won't be coming back."

Paul drained the last of his coffee and sat silently for a moment. "And Gunther? Will he be staying on at Fairmont?"

"Only until the school year ends in June. At the hospital, he told Magda and me he intends to take early retirement and use his carpentry skills to become an entrepreneur. We heartily encouraged him to do so."

Paul was momentarily silent.

"And what about Elaine? Will she be retiring too?"

"I don't know, but I think so. We all swore to her we would never reveal the story of how her cherished coaster got into Principal Morris's office, so really, there's no *need* for her to leave. But, personally, I think the whole affair—no pun intended—left a sour taste in her mouth, and I wouldn't be surprised if she has had enough of teaching and decides to see the world while she still can.

Paul crossed his arms in front of his chest and leaned back in his chair. "That would be great," he said sincerely. "A fine lady like that should have some fun, and a change of scenery would no doubt be therapeutic for her."

"*Therapeutic?*" Julie's eyebrows shot up. "So, tell me, Detective, what would be therapeutic for you? A train ride across the Rockies? A cruise in the Caribbean?"

Paul smiled softly. "Me? I'm a home loving guy, and I live for my job. Catching bad guys and putting them away; that's what does it for me."

"You want to make the world a safer place? Is that it? Is that what does it for you?" Her eyes were laughing, but they were serious as well.

"If I can. Yes." He studied her silently for a second. "So, Julie, it's your turn. You tell me—what does it for you?"

She thought about it carefully. "Well, teaching English to high schoolers is at the top of my list and…" She hesitated.

"And?"

"And having coffee with guys like you."

Paul was taken aback by the sudden change of direction in their conversation. This was a sharp girl. Sharp and surprisingly unpredictable. She could prove to be a challenge, but some risks are worth taking. He looked intently across the table.

"*Guys* like me? Could you be more specific?" He stifled a smile. "Maybe name names?"

"Yes, I could… if you would like," she said innocently.

"I think I would like that very much." He reached across the table and lightly closed his hand over hers.

She let the moment linger just long enough to tighten the tension between them. Then she slowly slid her hand out from under his and softly stroked the tops of his fingers.

"So would I, Paul," she said, her voice strong and full of conviction. "So would I."

THE END

Printed in Canada